EMIL
AND THE
DETECTIVES

Erich Kästner

translated by May Massee
illustrated by Walter Trier

AN
APPLE®
PAPERBACK

SCHOLASTIC INC.
New York Toronto London Auckland Sydney

ISBN 0-590-40571-3

12 11 10 9 8 7 6 5 4   1 2 3 4 5/9

Printed in the U.S.A.   40

Contents

About the Names in This Book

This book was originally written in German. It was translated into English by May Massee. The translator thought you might like to know something about the German names, so she included the following explanation.

In the story about Emil, we think Mr. Kästner, the author, has entertained himself in naming his people. Some of the names have no special meaning, but some of them have — and they all have a good German sound. So we left the names just as they are in the German version:

HERR is *Mr.*

FRAU is *Mrs.*

FRÄU-LEIN is *Miss.*

EMIL is pronounced *ay-meel.*

TISCH-BEIN means *Table-leg.*

FRAU FRI-SEU-SE TISCH-BEIN is supposed to be rather elegant. FRISEUSE is a French word that means *Hairdresser.*

KLEM-NER-MEI-STER means *Master-plumber.*

PONY HÜT-CHEN means *Pony Little-cap* — a pet name, of course. She *is* sort of staunch like a pony, and rather saucy.

MÜLLER is *Miller.*

BÄC-KER-MEI-STER WIRTH is really two names, like a hyphenated name. *Bäckermeister* means *Master baker,* and *Wirth* means *Landlord* — naturally a very important person.

NAU-MANN is *Newman.*

FLEISCH-ER-MEI-STER is *Head-butcher.*

GRUND-EIS is *Ground-ice.*

KURZ-HALS is *Short-neck.*

NEU-STADT is *New-city.*

DIENS-TAG is *Tuesday* and means *service day* or a kind of *office day,* so you'll see that little Dienstag was well named.

KRUMM-BIEGEL means *Bandy-legged.*

STUHL-BEIN means *Chair-leg.*

FISCH-BEIN means *Fish-leg.*

ÜBER-BEIN means *Extra-leg.*

These would not sound like names if they were translated. In German, they do sound like ordinary names; but when you stop to think what they mean, you can't help smiling a little. They're a sort of joke on German names.

But the Story Does Not Begin Yet...

First: Emil himself

First of all, here is Emil himself. In his dark-blue Sunday suit. He doesn't care much about wearing it and only puts it on when he has to. Blue clothes do get spotted so easily— and then Emil's mother dampens the clothesbrush, holds the boy between her knees, and scrubs and brushes while she says, "Tut, tut, you know I can't buy you another suit." And then Emil remembers when it's too late that his mother works all day long so that they can have enough to eat and Emil can go to school.

Second: Frau Friseuse Tischbein, Emil's mother

When Emil was five years old, his father died. He was Herr Klempnermeister Tischbein. Since then Emil's mother has dressed people's hair. And waved it. And shampooed the shopgirls and the married women of the neighborhood. Besides that she has to cook and keep her house in order and do all her own washing. She is very fond of Emil and is glad that she can work and earn money. Sometimes she sings gay little songs. Sometimes she is ill, and Emil cooks fried eggs for her and for himself. He can do that. He can fry steak, too, with breadcrumbs and onions.

The train this coach belongs to travels to Berlin. And probably in this compartment, in the next chapters, strange things will happen. A compartment like this is a curious contrivance. Perfect strangers sit here, and in a couple of hours they are as friendly as if they had known each other for years. Sometimes that's very nice and pleasant. But sometimes it isn't. For who knows what sort of people they all are?

Fourth: The man in the stiff hat

No one knows him. Of course, as a rule, you should think the best of anyone until you know something to prove the contrary. But in this connection I must beg of you to be a little cautious. Because, as they say, "Foresight is better than hindsight." Man is good, they say. Well, that is true. But you'd better not take him too much for granted, this good man. Because he might suddenly become bad.

Fifth: Pony Hütchen, Emil's cousin

The little one on the little bicycle is Emil's cousin from Berlin. In the main, Pony Hütchen is a charming child, and of course her real name is something quite different. Her mother and Frau Tischbein are sisters. And Pony Hütchen is only a nickname.

Sixth: The hotel on Nollendorf Place

Nollendorf Place is in Berlin. And if I am not mistaken, on Nollendorf Place is the hotel where several people of this story meet each other without shaking hands at all. The hotel might be on Wittenberg Place, as far as that goes. Perhaps even on Fehrbelliner Place. In other words, I know just exactly where it is! But the manager came to me when he heard that I was going to write a book about what happened there, and said that I must not tell you the name of the Place. Because, he said, obviously it wouldn't be a recommendation for his hotel if it were known that "such people" had spent the night there. I saw right away what he meant. And then he went off again.

Seventh: The boy with the automobile horn

Gustav is his name. And in gym work he has a straight A. What else has he? A good kind heart and an automobile horn. All the boys in the fourth grade know him and treat him as if he were their president. When he runs through the neighborhood honking his horn, the children drop everything and tear downstairs to see what's up. Usually he just wants to get enough boys for two football teams, and they all go off to the playground. But sometimes the horn serves quite different purposes. As, for instance, in the affair with Emil.

Eighth: The little branch bank

In all parts of the city the big banks have their branch offices. There, if you have an account, you can cash checks. Sometimes, too, the apprentices and messenger girls come to change ten marks into a hundred tenpenny pieces so their cashiers can have small change. And whoever wants to can have dollars or French francs or Italian lire changed into German money here. Even at night people sometimes come to the bank, although there is no one there to wait on them. So they have to help themselves.

Ninth: Emil's grandmother

She is the jolliest old grandmother I know. Yet she has had nothing but worries all her life long. Some people don't have any trouble at all to keep cheerful. For others it's a strenuous and serious business. She used to live with Emil's parents. But when Herr Tischbein died she went to her other daughter's, in Berlin, because Emil's mother did not earn enough for three people to live on. Now the old women lives in Berlin. And every letter she writes ends with this: "I am well and hope you are the same."

Tenth: The composing room of a great paper

Everything that happens gets into the paper. Only it must be just a bit out of the ordinary. If a calf has four legs, naturally no one is interested. But if she has five or six—and that does happen—then the grownups want to read about it for breakfast. If Herr Müller is an exemplary citizen, no one wants to know anything about him. But if Herr Müller puts water in the milk and sells the stuff for sweet cream, then he gets into the paper no matter what he may do to prevent it.

Have you ever passed a newspaper building at night? It rattles and rings and rumbles and the walls shake.

There! Now, at last, we will begin!

First Chapter

Emil Helps to Shampoo

"THERE!" said Frau Tischbein. "Now, just follow me with that pitcher of hot water." She herself took another pitcher and the little blue jug with the liquid camomile soap and walked out of the kitchen into the living room. Emil took up his pitcher and followed his mother.

In the living room sat a woman with her head bent over the white washbowl. Her hair was undone and hung down like three pounds of wool. Emil's mother poured the liquid camomile soap over the woman's blond hair and rubbed the strange head until it foamed.

"Is it too hot?" she said.

"Well, it will do," replied the head.

"Oh, that's Frau Bäckermeister Wirth. How do you

do?" said Emil and shoved his pitcher under the wash-stand.

"You're lucky, Emil. I hear you are going to Berlin," remarked the head. And it sounded as if whoever was speaking was buried in whipped cream.

"At first he hardly wanted to go," said his mother, rubbing busily at Frau Wirth's head. "But why should a boy kill all his time here? He has never seen Berlin. And my sister Martha has invited us for a visit again and again. Her husband earns good money. He is in the post office. Inside work. Of course, I can't go with him. Before the holidays there is so much to do. But he is big enough, and he must learn to look out for himself. And besides, my mother is meeting him at the Fried-richstrasse Station. They will pick him up at the flower stand."

"He's bound to like Berlin. It's just made for children. We were there a year and half ago with the bowling club. Such a din! There are actually streets there that are just as bright at night as they are in the daytime. And the automobiles!" informed Frau Wirth from the depths of the washbowl.

"A good many foreign cars?" asked Emil.

"How should I know about that?" answered Frau Wirth, and had to sneeze. She'd got some soapsuds up her nose.

"There, run along and get yourself ready," urged his mother. "I've laid out your good suit in the bedroom.

Put it on so that we can eat as soon as I've done up Frau Wirth's hair."

"What shirt shall I wear?" Emil wanted to know.

"Everything is lying on the bed. And pull your stockings up carefully. And first wash yourself thoroughly. And put new laces in your shoes. Trot along, now!"

"Oh heck!" remarked Emil, and strolled off.

When Frau Wirth had left, all beautifully waved and pleased with her looks in the mirror, Emil's mother went into the bedroom and found her son wandering about dejectedly.

"Who invented best suits anyway, can you tell me that?"

"No, I'm sorry. But why do you want to know?"

"Give me his address, and I'll shoot the bird!"

"It's too bad about you. Other children are unhappy because they haven't any good suit. We all have our troubles. . . . Before I forget it — tonight be sure to ask Aunt Martha for a coat hanger, and hang up your suit carefully. First it must be brushed, though. Don't forget that. And in the morning you can wear your sweater again and this old jacket. Now, what else? The suitcase is packed. The flowers for Aunt Martha are done up. The money for Grandmother I'll give you later. And now we'll eat. Come, young man!"

Frau Tischbein put her arm around Emil's shoulder and steered him toward the kitchen. There was macaroni with ham and grated Parmesan cheese. Emil ate like a farmhand. Only once in a while he sat back and looked over at his mother as if he feared she might think he had too good an appetite when he was going away so soon.

"And send me a card right away. I put one where you can find it in the suitcase, on top."

"Sure thing," said Emil, and scraped a bit of macaroni off his knee as quietly as possible. Fortunately his mother didn't notice anything.

"Give them all my love. And keep your eyes open. In Berlin things are very different from Neustadt. On Sunday you will go with Uncle Robert to the Kaiser Friedrich Museum. And remember your manners, so that people won't think that we don't know how to behave."

"You can trust me," said Emil.

Dinner over, they went into the sitting room. His mother took a tin box from the cupboard and counted out some money. Then she shook her head and counted it again. Then she asked, "Who was here yesterday afternoon anyway, hm?"

"Fräulein Thomas," answered Emil, "and Frau Homburg."

"Yes, but still it doesn't come out right." She thought a minute, looked over the piece of paper where she had jotted down her receipts, did some arithmetic, and finally announced, "It's eight marks short."

"The gas man was here this morning."

"Sure enough. Now it comes out right, worse luck." She gave a little whistle, probably of vexation over her worries, and took three bank notes out of the tin box. "There, Emil! There are a hundred and forty marks. A hundred and twenty for you to give to Grandmother, and twenty for you. Tell Grandmother not to blame me for not sending it before, but I would have run too short. That's why you are bringing more than usual this time. And give her a kiss. Understand? The twenty marks left over are for you. You can buy your return ticket out of that when you're coming home. That will leave you about ten marks. I'm not just sure. Out of the rest you can pay for what you eat or drink when you go out. Besides, it's always a good thing to have a few extra marks in your pocket that you don't need at the moment. Then you're all right, whatever happens. There! And here is the envelope from Aunt Martha's letter. I'll put the notes in here. And be careful not to lose it. What will you do with it?"

She placed the three notes in the neatly opened envelope, folded it in the middle, and gave it to Emil.

Emil thought hard for a minute. Then he put it in his right inside pocket way down, patted himself on the outside of his blue coat to make sure, and announced with conviction, "There, that won't climb out."

"And don't tell anybody on the train that you have so much money with you."

"But Mother!" Emil was hurt. To accuse him of such stupidity!

Frau Tischbein put some more money into her pocketbook. Then she took the tin box back to the cupboard and hastily read over the letter from her sister in Berlin giving the exact time of the departure and arrival of Emil's train. . . .

Probably many of you will think that no one need make such a fuss over a hundred and forty marks as Frau Tischbein was making for Emil's benefit. And if a person earned two thousand or twenty thousand or maybe a hundred thousand marks a month, of course he wouldn't have to.

But in case you don't know it — most people earn far less than that. And whether you like it or not, anyone who earns thirty-five marks a week must think that a hundred and forty marks he has saved is a great deal of money. For lots of people a hundred marks is almost as much as a million. You might say that they write 100 with six ciphers, and how much a million really is they cannot imagine even in their dreams.

Emil had no father. So his mother had to dress hair in her sitting room, wash blond heads and brown heads, and work endlessly to have enough to eat and to pay for gas and coal and the rent and clothes and books and school. Only once in a while she was ill and stayed in bed. Then the doctor would come and prescribe medicine. And then Emil would make hot compresses for his mother and cook for them both. And when she was asleep, Emil would mop up the floor with wet flannel rags so that she wouldn't say, "I must get up. The house is going to rack and ruin."

I hope you'll understand and not laugh when I tell you that Emil was a model boy. You see he loved his mother. And he would have been ashamed to death if he had been lazy while she worked and reckoned and worked again. So how could he loaf on his schoolwork or crib from Richard Naumann? How could he skip school even if he had a chance? He saw her tire herself out so that he would not have to do without anything the other school children had. How could he cheat her and give her trouble?

Emil was a model boy. There it is. But he wasn't one of the sort that can't be anything else because they're cowards and stingy and not real boys. He was a model boy because he wanted to be. He had made a resolution, the way people make resolutions not to go to the movies any more, or not to eat any more candy. He had made the resolution, and sometimes it was very hard for him to keep it.

But when he went home at Easter and could say, "Mother, here are my grades, and I am the highest again," then he was very happy. He liked the praise he got in school and everywhere — not for himself, but because it made his mother happy. He was proud that in his own way he could pay back a little of what she had been doing for him his whole life long.

"Gracious!" said his mother, "we must get to the station. It's quarter past one. And the train leaves a little before two."

"All right, let's go, Frau Tischbein," said Emil to his mother, "but I want you to notice that I'm carrying my suitcase myself."

Second Chapter

Policeman Jeschke
Keeps Still

IN FRONT OF THE HOUSE, Emil's mother said, "If the horsecar comes we'll ride to the station."

Which one of you knows how a horsecar looks? As it is coming round the corner and stopping because Emil waves to it, I will describe it for you quickly before it goes rattling off again.

Well — first of all, the horsecar is a crazy thing. It runs on rails like a real streetcar, but there is just an old cab horse hitched to the front of it. For Emil and his friends the old cab horse was simply a disgrace, and they dreamed of electric cars with wires overhead and underneath, and five spotlights in the front, and three in the rear. Only the Mayor of Neustadt thought that the four-mile run could be made well enough with one living horsepower. Up to now there had been no talk of electricity, and the driver had nothing to do with steering wheels and levers. Instead he held the reins in his left hand and the whip in his right. Giddap!

And if a man lived at 12 Town Hall Street and he sat in the horsecar and wished to get out, he simply knocked on the glass. Then the driver went, "Whoa!" and the traveler was home. The real stop was perhaps in front of Number 30 or 46. But that didn't matter to the Neustadt Streetcar Company. It had time. The horse had time. The driver had time. The Neustadt citizens had time. And if anyone happened to be in a special hurry he went on foot. . . .

At the railway station Frau Tischbein and her son got out. And while Emil was fishing his bag off the platform a deep voice boomed behind them, "Well, you must be going to Switzerland."

That was the Chief of Police, Jeschke. Emil's mother answered, "No, my boy is going to relatives in Berlin for a week." Everything turned suddenly dark blue, almost black, before Emil's eyes. Because he had a very guilty conscience. Recently a dozen of the schoolboys on the way home from gymnastics on the river meadow had jammed an old felt hat down on the cool head of the monument to the Grand Duke, the one called Karl Crooked Face. And then Emil, because he could draw well, had been boosted up by the others and had to paint a red nose and a pitch-black mustache with colored crayons on the face of the Grand Duke! And while he was painting, Officer Jeschke had turned up on the other end of the square.

The boys had torn off like lightning. But there was the danger that he had recognized them.

However, he said nothing, but wished Emil a pleasant journey and then inquired of his mother — about the state of her health and her business.

In spite of that Emil was not quite at ease. As he was carrying his bag across the square to the station he was weak in the knees. And every minute he feared that Officer Jeschke would growl out suddenly behind him, "Emil Tischbein, you are arrested. Hands up!" But nothing at all happened. Perhaps the officer was just going to wait until Emil came back?

Then his mother bought a ticket at the window, a third-class ticket, naturally, and a platform ticket for herself. And they went to Track Number 1 — Neustadt Station has four tracks, if you please — and waited for the train to Berlin. There were only a few minutes left.

"Don't leave anything, dear! And don't sit on the flowers. You can ask someone to lift your suitcase up into the baggage rack. But be polite about it and say, 'Please.'"

"I'll get my suitcase up myself. I'm no baby."

"All right, then. Don't forget to get out. You'll be in Berlin at six seventeen. At the Friedrichstrasse Station.

Don't get off before that, at the Zoo Station or some other."

"Have no fear, young woman."

"And above all, don't be as fresh with other people as you are with your mother. Don't throw the paper on the floor when you eat your sandwiches — and — don't lose your money!"

Emil clutched his coat and dived into his right-hand breast pocket. Then he breathed a sigh of relief and murmured, "All safe."

He took his mother's arm and walked with her up and down the platform.

"And don't overwork, Mother! And don't get sick! You would have nobody to take care of you. I'd take a flying machine on the spot and come home. And write me once in a while. And I'll stay a week at the most, you know that." Emil hugged his mother close, and she gave him a kiss on his nose.

Then the train for Berlin came thundering in and stopped. Emil gave his mother just another little squeeze and climbed up into a compartment with his suitcase in his hand. His mother handed him his bouquet and his package of sandwiches, and asked if he'd found a seat. He nodded.

"Good, get off at Friedrichstrasse!"

He nodded.

"And your grandmother will be waiting at the flower-stand."

He nodded.

"And take care, you young rascal."

He nodded.

"And be nice to Pony Hütchen. You probably won't know each other at all!"

He nodded.

"And write me."

"You me, too."

And so probably it would have gone on for hours if there hadn't been any timetable. The conductor with the red leather bag shouted, "All aboard! All aboard!" The doors clanged shut. The engine pulled out. And off they went.

The mother waved her handkerchief for a long time. Then she turned around slowly and went home. And because she had her handkerchief ready in her hand, as it were, she wept a few tears into it.

But not for long. Because at home Frau Fleischermeister Augustin was waiting, and she wanted a good thorough shampoo.

Third Chapter

The Trip to Berlin
Can Start

E MIL TOOK OFF HIS CAP and said, "How do you do? Maybe there's an empty seat here?" Of course there was an empty seat. And a fat woman who had taken off her left shoe because it pinched said to her neighbor, a man who puffed frightfully at every breath, "Such polite children are rare nowadays. When I think back on my childhood — my goodness, what a different spirit there was then." And she wiggled her pinched toes in her left stocking in time with her talking. Emil looked on with interest. And the man could hardly nod for his puffing.

Emil had known for a long time that there are always people who say, "Ah well, things used to be much better." So he paid no attention when anyone announced that formerly the air was much more health-ful or that the oxen had bigger heads. Because usually what they said wasn't true, and they belonged to the sort who refuse to be satisfied with things as they are for fear of becoming contented.

Emil felt his right breast pocket and was relieved when he heard the envelope crackle. His traveling companions all looked like trustworthy people, and not like robbers or murderers. Next to the man who puffed so sat a woman who was crocheting a shawl. And by the window near Emil a man in a stiff hat was reading the newspaper.

Suddenly he laid the paper aside, took from his pocket a bar of chocolate, held it out to the boy, and said, "Well, young man, want some?"

"Thank you very much," answered Emil and took the chocolate. Then he hastily took off his cap, as an after-thought, made a little bow, and said, "Emil Tischbein is my name."

The passengers laughed. The man, for his part, sol-emnly lifted his hat and said, "Very pleased, my name's Grundeis!"

Then the fat woman who had taken off her left shoe asked him, "Does Shopkeeper Kurzhals still live in Neustadt?"

"Yes indeed, Herr Kurzhals still lives there," Emil informed her. "Do you know him? He has bought the lot where his store is."

"Well, well. Tell him Frau Jakob from Gross-Grünau wanted to be remembered to him."

"But I'm going to Berlin."

"It will be time enough when you get back," said Frau Jakob. She wiggled her toes again and laughed until her hat fell over her face.

"So you're going to Berlin?" asked Herr Grundeis.

"Yes, and my grandmother is waiting at the flower stand in the Friedrichstrasse Station," answered Emil, and felt his breast pocket. Thank goodness, the envelope crackled again as before.

"Have you ever been to Berlin?"

"No."

"Well, it will astonish you! In Berlin nowadays there are houses a hundred stories high, and they have to fasten the roofs to the sky so they won't blow away. And if a man is in a great hurry to go to another part of the city they clap him into a chest at the post office, pop it into a tube, and shoot it like a pneumatic letter to the post office of the section where he wants to go.

"And if you haven't any money you go to a bank and leave your brains as a pledge, and you get a thousand marks. Naturally, you can't buy them back from the bank unless you pay them twelve hundred marks. And now some wonderful medical appliances have been invented and ——"

"It's plain to see that you have left your brains at the

bank," said the man who puffed so horribly to the man with the stiff hat. "Quit your nonsense."

The toes of the fat woman stood still in awe, and the woman who was crocheting held her breath.

Emil laughed uncertainly. And a long argument started between the men. Emil thought, "I should worry," and got out his sandwiches, even though he had just eaten his dinner. As he was eating his third sandwich the train stopped at a station. Emil could not see the sign, and he didn't understand what the guard shouted at the window. Most of the passengers got out — the puffing man, the crocheting woman, and also Frau Jakob. She was almost too late because she couldn't get her shoe on.

"Well, remember me to Herr Kurzhals," she said again, and Emil nodded.

And then he and the man with the stiff hat were left alone. Emil was not very well pleased at that. A man who divides his chocolate with you and tells you crazy stories is pretty queer. Emil wanted to feel his envelope again for a change. But he didn't dare. Instead he went into the toilet as the train started on, took the envelope out of his pocket, and counted the money. It was all there, and then he did not know what to do. Finally he had an idea. He took a pin that he found in his lapel, stuck it first through the three notes, next through the envelope, and finally through the lining of

Herr Grundeis slept and snored a bit.

his jacket. You might say that he nailed the money tight. "There," he thought, "now nothing can happen." And then he went back into the compartment.

Herr Grundeis had made himself snug in a corner and slept. Emil was glad he didn't have to talk and looked out of the window. Trees, windmills, fields, factories, herds of cows, and waving peasants all went by. And it was nice to see how they all whirled around just as if they were on a phonograph record. But you can't stare out of a window forever.

Herr Grundeis slept on and on and snored a bit. Emil wanted to walk up and down, but if he did he might wake the man, and he didn't care to do that at all. So he leaned back in the opposite corner of the compartment and watched the sleeping man. Why did he always keep his hat on? He had a rather long face and a tiny black mustache and a hundred wrinkles around his mouth, and his ears were very thin and stuck out from his head.

Whoop! Emil shook himself and was terrified. He had almost fallen asleep. He didn't dare do that under any circumstances. If only even one other person would get on. The train stopped several times, but no one came. It was only four o'clock, and Emil still had more than two hours to ride. He pinched his legs. That always helped in school when Herr Bremser gave the history lesson.

It worked for a while. Emil wondered how Pony

Hütchen looked now. But he couldn't remember her face. He only knew that on her last visit, when she and Grandmother and Aunt Martha were in Neustadt, Pony had wanted to box with him. Naturally, he had refused, because she was a lightweight and he was at least a welterweight. It would have been unfair, he said. And if he were to give her an uppercut they would have to peel her down from the wall. But she wouldn't let him alone until Aunt Martha interfered.

Zowie! He almost fell off the seat. Asleep again? He pinched and pinched his legs. He must have black and blue spots all over already. And still it didn't do any good.

He tried counting buttons. He counted down and then up again. Counting down there were twenty-three buttons, and counting up there were twenty-four. Emil leaned back and pondered over how that could be.

And he fell sound asleep.

Fourth Chapter

A Dream in Which
There Is Much Running

SUDDENLY IT SEEMED TO Emil that the train was
going around in a circle, just as the toy trains do
that children play with. He looked out of the window
and found it most curious. The circle was getting
smaller and smaller. The engine was coming nearer and
nearer to the last car. And it seemed as if it were doing
that on purpose. The train turned around on itself just
like a dog that tries to bite his own tail. And inside
that black racing circle were trees and a glass windmill
and a great house with two hundred stories.

Emil wanted to know what time it was and started
to pull his watch out of his pocket. He pulled and
pulled, and finally it was the big grandfather clock out
of his mother's room. He looked at the face, and there

it said, "185 miles an hour. It is forbidden on penalty of your life to spit on the floor!" He looked out of the window again. The engine was coming nearer and nearer to the last car. And he was terribly worried. Because if the engine struck the last car naturally there would be a train wreck. That was clear. Emil did not want to wait for that on any account. He opened the door and ran along the outside steps. Perhaps the engineer had gone to sleep? Emil looked through the windows of the compartments as he worked his way along. There was no one sitting anywhere. The train was empty. Emil saw only one man, who had on a stiff hat made of chocolate. The man broke off a big piece from his hat brim and gulped it down. Emil rapped on the windowpane and pointed at the engine. But the man only laughed, broke himself another big piece of chocolate, and patted himself on the stomach because it tasted so good.

Finally Emil got to the coal car. Then he clambered up to the engineer's cabin. The engineer was hunched up on a coachman's seat, whirling his whip and holding the reins as if there were horses hitched in front of the train. And that's just what there were! Six pairs of horses dragged the train. They had silver roller skates on their hoofs, and they flew along over the rails singing, "Must I go, must I go to that city so far?"

Emil shook the coachman and shouted, "Pull up

your horses, or you'll have an accident." Then he saw that the coachman was none other than Officer Jeschke.

He gave Emil a piercing glance and shouted, "Who were the other youngsters? Who painted up the Grand Duke Karl?"

"Me," said Emil.

"Who else?"

"That I won't tell!"

"Then we'll keep right on going in a circle!"

And Officer Jeschke whipped up his steeds so that they reared up and flew faster than ever toward the last car. And in the last car sat Frau Jakob, brandishing the shoes in her hand and frightened to death because the horses were already snapping at her toes.

"I'll give you twenty marks, Officer," shouted Emil.

"Please stop such nonsense!" shrieked Jeschke and plied his whip on the horses as if he were possessed.

Emil couldn't bear it any longer, he jumped off the train. He turned twenty somersaults of the way down, but it didn't hurt him. He stood up and looked back at the train. It was standing still, and the twelve horses turned their heads toward Emil. Officer Jeschke had sprung up and was whipping his horses and bellowing, "Up there and after him!" And then the twelve horses sprang off the tracks and sprinted after Emil, and the cars hopped about like rubber balls.

Emil wasted no time, but ran away as fast as he could. Over a meadow, past many trees, through a brook, toward the skyscraper. Every now and then he looked behind him. The train thundered on with no letup. It knocked the trees right and left and split them to pieces. Only one old oak was left standing, and on its topmost branch sat fat Frau Jakob, swaying in the wind and weeping because she couldn't get her shoe on. Emil ran on.

In the house that was two hundred stories high there was a great black door. He ran in, through the house, and out the other side. The train followed after. Emil would much rather have sat himself down in a corner to sleep, for he was fearfully tired and trembling in every limb. But he dared not go to sleep. The train was already rattling through the house.

Emil saw an iron ladder. It went up the house way to the roof. He began to climb. Luckily he was good at gym work. While he climbed he counted the stories. At the fiftieth floor he risked turning around. The trees had grown very small, and the glass windmill was hardly recognizable. But oh, horrors! the train was running right up, up the side of the house. Emil climbed higher and higher. And the train snorted and clumped up the ladder rungs just as if they were tracks.

The 100th floor, 120th, 140th, 160th, 180th, 190th, 200th floor. Emil stood on the roof and had no idea what to do next. He could hear the neighing of the horses. Then the boy ran to the other end of the roof, took his handkerchief out of his pocket, and spread it

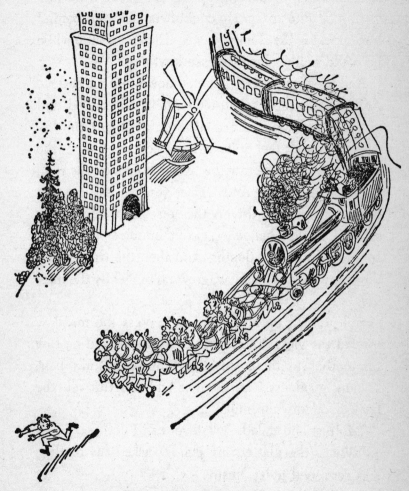

Emil ran away as fast as he could.

out. And as the sweating horses came creeping over the edge of the roof with the train after them Emil stretched his handkerchief high above his head and sprang off into space. He could hear the train behind him knocking the chimneys over. Then for a little while he could neither hear nor see anything.

And then, crash! He plumped down into a meadow. At first he lay there exhausted with his eyes closed, and would have liked to dream a beautiful dream. But because he didn't feel quite safe yet he looked up at the house, and there he saw the twelve horses on the roof, opening umbrellas. And Officer Jeschke had an umbrella too, and was driving the horses on with it. They sat back on their haunches, gave themselves a jerk, and sprang off into the depths. And then the train sailed down toward the meadow, growing bigger by the minute.

Emil jumped up again and ran across the meadow toward the glass mill. It was transparent, and he saw his mother in there washing Frau Augustin's hair. "Thank goodness!" he thought and ran through the back door into the mill.

"Mother," he called, "whatever can I do?"

"What's the matter, my child?" asked his mother, and scrubbed away busily.

"Look through the wall!"

Frau Tischbein looked out just in time to see the

train and the horses land in the meadow and come tearing across to the mill.

"Why, that is Officer Jeschke," said his mother, and shook her head in astonishment.

"He has been chasing after me the whole time like mad."

"Well, what in the world?"

"A while ago I painted a red nose and a mustache on the Grand Duke Karl Crooked Face in the market place."

"Yes, and where else should you paint mustaches?" asked Frau Augustin, and sneezed violently.

"Nowhere else, Frau Augustin. But that isn't the worst. He wants to know who else was there. And that I can't tell him. That's a question of honor."

"Emil is right about that," agreed his mother, "but what shall we do?"

"Put on the motor, dear Frau Tischbein," said Frau Augustin.

Emil's mother pushed down a lever that was underneath the table. The windmill sails began to turn, and as they were made of glass and the sun was shining on them, they shimmered and shone so that one could hardly bear to look at them.

And the twelve horses running with their train became so frightened that they shied and reared up and refused to take another step. Officer Jeschke swore so they could hear him through the glass walls. But the horses didn't stir from the spot.

"There, now we can wash my scalp in peace," said Frau Augustin. "Nothing more can happen to your boy."

Frau Tischbein accordingly went on with her work. Emil sat down on a chair that was also made of glass and whistled to himself. Then he laughed out loud and said, "This is marvelous. If I had known before that you were here I'd never have climbed up that blamed house."

"I hope you didn't tear your suit," said his mother. Then she asked, "Did you take good care of the money?"

At that Emil gave a great jump. And with a crash he fell off the glass chair.

And woke up.

Fifth Chapter

Emil Gets Off at the Wrong Station

A s EMIL AWOKE the train was just getting under way again. He had fallen off the seat in his sleep and was lying on the floor, frightened almost out of his wits without knowing why. His heart was beating like a trip hammer. There he squatted in the train and had almost forgotten where he was. Bit by bit it all came back to him. Right — he was going to Berlin. And he had fallen asleep. Just like the man in the stiff hat. . . .

Emil sat bolt upright with a jerk and whispered, "Why, he's gone off." His knees trembled. Very slowly he got up and mechanically brushed the dust off his suit. Then the next question was, "Is the money still there?" And at that question he felt an indescribable terror.

For a long time he stood leaning against the door, not daring to move. Just over there that man Grundeis had sat and slept and snored. And now he was gone. Of course, everything might be all right. It was absurd to be suspicious right away. Just because Emil was going to Friedrichstrasse Station in Berlin was no reason why everyone else had to go there too. And the money, of course, was safe in its proper place. First, it was in his pocket. Second, it was in the envelope. And third, it was fastened to the lining with a pin. And then he reached slowly into his right inside pocket.

The pocket was empty! The money was gone!

Emil burrowed around in his pocket with his left hand while he pushed and poked at it from the outside with his right hand. There was no doubt about it — the pocket was empty and the money was gone.

"Ouch!" Emil pulled his hand out of his pocket. And not only his hand, but in it the pin with which he had pinned the notes. Nothing but the pin was left. And that was pricking his left forefinger so that it bled.

He wound his handkerchief around the finger and began to cry. Naturally, not for that tiny bit of blood. Two weeks before he had run into a lamppost so hard that it was almost broken off, and Emil still had the bump on his forehead from it. And he hadn't cried one second.

He wept now about the money. And he wept because of his mother. Anyone who can't understand that, no matter how brave he may be, is beyond help. Emil knew how his mother had economized for months to save the hundred and forty marks for his grandmother and for his trip to Berlin. And hardly was her young son in the train before he settled himself back in the corner, dreamed a crazy dream, and allowed himself to be robbed by that pig of a man. Wasn't it enough to make him cry? What was he to do now? Get off in Berlin and say to his grandmother, "Here I am, but you might as well know you'll get no money? Instead you had better give me my train fare back to Neustadt. Otherwise I'll have to walk."

That was splendid! His mother had economized for nothing. His grandmother would not get a penny. He couldn't stay in Berlin. He dared not go back home. And all because of a rascal who gave chocolate to children and pretended to be asleep. And then he robbed them. Boy, oh boy! what a swell world it was!

Emil dried his tears and looked around.

If he pulled the bell cord the train would stop at once. And then a brakeman would come, and another, and still another. And they would all ask, "What's the matter?"

"My money is stolen," he would say.

"Another time take better care of it," they would answer. "Please get on again. Who are you? Where do you live? To pull the bell once costs a hundred marks. The bill will be sent."

In the express trains there are corridors so that you can run through the whole thing from one end to the other, even to the caboose, and report a burglary. But not in the third class! In such a stupid train! Here you must wait till the next station because you have to step off one car and walk along outside to get to the next car. And meantime the man with the stiff hat could be miles and miles away. Emil did not even know at what station he had got off. How late was it, anyway? When would they reach Berlin? Great houses and villas with gay gardens and then high dirty red chimneys ambled past the windows. Apparently this was Berlin already. At the next station he would have to call the guard and tell him all about it. And he would promptly notify the police.

Now, to top it all, he had to get mixed up with the police, and naturally Officer Jeschke could keep silent no longer but would have to admit officially, "I don't know why, but that schoolboy, Emil Tischbein of Neustadt, doesn't quite please me. First he daubs up noble monuments. And then he allows himself to be robbed of a hundred and forty marks. Perhaps they weren't stolen at all?

"A boy who daubs up monuments will tell lies. I have had experience with that. Probably he has buried the money in the woods or has swallowed it and plans to go to America with it? There's no sense trying to capture the thief — not the slightest. The boy Tischbein himself is the thief. Please, Chief of Police, arrest him."

Horrible! He could not even confide in the police!

He took his bag out of the rack, put on his cap, stuck the pin back in his coat lapel, and got ready to go. He had not the slightest idea what he would do. But stay another five minutes in this compartment he would not. That was certain.

Meanwhile the train was slowing down. Emil saw rows of tracks shining outside. Then they came into a station.

Some porters ran along by the car to get the baggage. The train stopped!

Emil looked out of the window and saw a sign high up over the tracks. It said "Zoological Gardens." The doors flew open. People climbed out of the compartments. Other people were waiting for them with outstretched arms.

Emil leaned way out of the window, looking for the conductor. Some distance off and almost hidden in a crowd of people, he saw a stiff black hat. If that were the thief? Perhaps after he stole Emil's money he did not get off the train but just went into another car?

In the next second Emil was standing on the platform. He put down his bag, climbed back into the train, because he had forgotten his bunch of flowers in the baggage rack, got out again, picked up his bag in a hurry, and ran as fast as he could to the exit.

Where was the stiff hat? The boy stumbled over

people's legs, banged into someone with his suitcase, and ran on. The crowd was getting thicker and harder to press through.

There! There was the stiff hat! Good heavens, over there was another! Emil could hardly carry his bag. He wished he could leave it right there. But if he did probably that, too, would be stolen.

Finally he got up close to the stiff hat.

That must be the one. Was it?

No.

There was the next one.

No. That man was too small.

Emil wound himself in and out of the crowd like an Indian.

There, there!

That was the fellow. Thank goodness! That was Grundeis. He was just pushing through the gate and seemed to be in a hurry.

"Just wait, you beast," growled Emil, "we'll get you!" Then he gave up his ticket, took his bag in the other hand, clamped his flowers under his right arm, and ran downstairs behind the man.

Now it's do or die!

Sixth Chapter

Streetcar Line 177

E MIL WISHED he could run up to the fellow, post himself in front of him, and shout, "Give me my money!" But he didn't look as though he would answer, "Gladly, my good boy. Here it is. I will surely not do it again." The affair was not as simple as that. For the moment the most important thing was not to let the man out of his sight.

Emil hid himself behind a tall and ample woman who was walking ahead of him and peered out from behind her, now to the right, now to the left, to make sure that the man was still in sight and not suddenly running off in another direction. Meanwhile the man had reached the main entrance of the station and was looking around him, scanning the crowd as if he were trying to find someone. Emil kept close behind the large lady and came nearer and nearer. What would happen now? Soon he would have to pass the man, and there would be an end to all the secrecy. Perhaps the lady would help him? But she surely would not believe him. And the thief would say, "Pardon me, madam, what gives you such an idea? Do I look as if I had to rob little children?" And then all the people around would look at the boy and cry, "That is the limit! Lies about the grownups. Boys today are altogether too impudent." Emil's teeth were chattering already.

Fortunately, just then the man turned his head away again and stepped out into the open. Quick as a flash Emil jumped behind the door, put down his bag, and peered out of the window grating. Heavens! how his arm ached!

The thief crossed the street slowly, looked backward once more, and then walked on, apparently reassured. Then from the left came a streetcar and trailer, Number 177, and stopped. The man hesitated a second, stepped into the front car, and seated himself at a window.

Emil grabbed his bag again, ducked past the door, down the corridor, out of another door onto the street, and reached the trailer from behind just as the car was starting again. He threw his bag up, climbed after it, shoved it into a corner, placed himself in front of it, and took a deep breath. So that was over!

But what now? If the other got off on the way the

money would be gone for good. Because it wouldn't do to jump off with his bag. That would be too dangerous.

These autos! They rushed past the streetcar, honked and squeaked, signaled for left turns and right, and swung around corners; other autos pushed right after them. What a jam! And so many people on the sidewalks! And from every side street, cars, delivery carts, double-decker buses! Newsstands on every corner. Wonderful show windows with flowers, fruits, books, gold watches, clothes, and silk underwear. And tall, tall buildings.

So that was Berlin.

Emil would have liked to observe it all in peace. But there was no time for that. In the forward car sat a man who had Emil's money, who might get off at any moment and disappear in the crowd. Then Emil might as well give up. Because out there among the cars and the people and the motor buses you couldn't find anyone again. Emil stuck his head out. What if the fellow were gone already? Then he alone would be riding on — he didn't know where, he didn't know why. And meanwhile his grandmother was waiting at the Friedrichstrasse Station at the flower stall and had no notion that her grandson was careering across Berlin on Line Number 177 and was in great trouble.

It was maddening.

The car stopped for the first time. Emil kept his eyes on the forward car. But no one got off. Just a crowd of new passengers streamed into the car. They tramped past Emil too. One man grumbled because the boy had his head stuck out in the way.

"Don't you see that people want to get on?" he growled.

The guard who was selling tickets in the car pulled a cord. The bell rang. And the cars went on farther. Emil got back in his corner, was squeezed, and had his feet stepped on, and all of a sudden was terrified to think, "I have no money! When the conductor comes back here I'll have to buy a ticket. And if I can't buy one he'll put me off. And then I might as well be buried."

He looked over the people standing around. Could he twitch one of them by the coat and say, "Please lend me money for my fare"? Oh dear, they all had such solemn faces. One was reading a paper. A couple of others were talking about a great bank robbery. "They dug a regular tunnel," one of the men was saying, "and working from that they cleared out all the bank vaults. The loss probably amounted to several millions."

"It's almost impossible to determine what was really in the vaults," said the second, "because the people who rent the safe-deposit boxes do not have to tell the bank what is locked up in them."

"Yes, some people would declare that they had diamonds worth a hundred thousand marks when in reality they had only a bunch of worthless paper or a dozen plated spoons." And both of them chuckled.

"That's just what will happen to me," thought Emil sadly. "I will say, 'Herr Grundeis stole a hundred and forty marks from me,' and nobody will believe me. The thief will say I am just being impudent and it was only three and a half marks! What a nasty fix!"

The conductor was coming nearer and nearer the door. He was already standing in the doorway and calling, "Tickets?"

He tore off long white strips of paper and made rows of holes with a punch. The people on the platform gave him money and got their tickets.

"Now, you?" he questioned the boy.

"I lost my money, Conductor," answered Emil. Because no one would have believed about the robbery.

"Lost your money? I know that one. And where do you want to go?"

"I — I — don't know yet," stammered Emil.

"So? Well, you get off at the next station and find out where you want to go."

"Oh no, that won't do. I must stay here, Conductor, please."

"If I tell you to get off, you get off. Understand?"

"Give the youngster a ticket!" said the man who had been reading the paper. He gave money to the conductor. And the conductor gave the ticket to Emil, saying to the man, "If you only knew how many young ones get on here every day with a story of forgetting their money. And then they laugh at us behind our backs."

"This one won't laugh at us," answered the man.

The conductor stepped back inside the car.

"Thank you very, very much," said Emil.

"Oh, that's all right!" answered the man and buried himself in his paper again.

Then the cars stopped once more. Emil leaned out to see if the man in the stiff hat got off. But there was nothing to see.

"Might I ask you for your address?" Emil asked the man.

"What for?"

"So I can give you back your money when I get some. I'm staying about a week in Berlin, so I could bring it to you. Tischbein is my name. Emil Tischbein from Neustadt."

"No," said the man. "The fare was a present, of course. Do you need anything more?"

"Oh no, indeed," exclaimed Emil. "I couldn't take anything more."

"All right," said the man and turned back to his paper again.

And the car went on. And stopped. And went on farther. Emil read the name of the beautiful broad street. Kaiser Avenue, it was. He went on without knowing where he was going. In the other car sat a thief. And perhaps there were other thieves sitting or standing in the car. No one paid any attention to him. To be sure, a stranger had given him a ticket. But now he was just reading his paper again!

The city was so big, and Emil was so small. And no one cared to know why he had no money and why he didn't know where he had to get off. Four million people lived in Berlin, and not one of them was interested in Emil Tischbein. No one wants to know about other people's troubles. Everyone is busy about his own cares and joys. And when anyone says, "I'm really sorry about that," he usually doesn't mean anything more than, "Oh, leave me alone!"

What was going to happen? Emil swallowed hard and felt very very much alone.

Seventh Chapter

Great Excitement in Schumann Street

W HILE EMIL WAS STANDING on streetcar Number 177, riding down Kaiser Avenue without knowing where he would land, his grandmother and Pony Hütchen, his cousin, were waiting for him at the Friedrichstrasse Station. They were standing at the flower stall, according to the agreement, and kept looking at the clock. Many people passed by, with trunks and chests and satchels and pocketbooks and bouquets. But Emil was not among them.

"Probably he's grown to be a big boy, don't you suppose?" asked Pony and pushed her shiny little bicycle back and forth. She really shouldn't have brought it. But she had teased about it so long that her grandmother had finally consented. "All right, take it along, you silly goose." So now the silly goose was in a good humor and thinking happily of Emil's respectful glance when he should see her bicycle. "He'll think it's pretty grand," she said, and was perfectly certain she was right.

The grandmother was getting worried. "I wish I knew what the matter is. It's already twenty minutes past six, and the train must have come in long ago."

They waited a few minutes more, and then her grandmother sent the little girl to inquire. Of course, Pony Hütchen took her bike with her.

"Can you tell me where the train from Neustadt is?" she asked the guard, who stood at the gate with a ticket punch and saw that everyone who wanted to pass had a ticket.

"Neustadt? Neustadt?" he considered. "Oh yes, six seventeen! That train came in long ago."

"Oh dear, that's a shame! You see, we're waiting at the flower stand for my cousin Emil."

"That's fine, that's fine," said the man.

"Why should it be fine, Inspector?" asked Pony curiously, and played with the bell on her bike.

The guard said nothing, but turned his back on the child. "Aren't you the bright boy?" said Pony, offended. "I hope I'll meet you again."

Several people laughed. The guard bit his lips angrily. And Pony trotted back to the flower stand.

"The train came in long ago, Grandmother."

"What could have happened?" worried the old woman. "If he hadn't started his mother would have telegraphed. Do you suppose he got off at the wrong station? But we wrote so carefully just what to do."

"I can't make head or tail of it," Pony declared, and looked important. "He surely got off at the wrong station. Boys are so stupid. I'll bet on it. You'll see that I'm right."

And because there was nothing else to do they waited again. Five minutes.

Another five minutes.

"But there is really no sense to this," Pony told her grandmother. "We can stand here till we're black in the face. I wonder if there's another flower stand?"

"You go look around, but don't stay long."

Pony took her bike again and inspected the station. There was no other flower stand. Then she pestered two innocent guards with questions and came back proudly.

"There," she said, "there are no more flower stands. That *would* be funny. What was I going to say? Oh yes, the next train arrives from Neustadt at a little after half-past eight. We might just as well go home. And on the stroke of eight I'll ride back here. If he isn't here by then, he'll get a red-hot letter from me."

"Pony, be more careful of your speech."

"Well, you might say, he'll get a cool letter from me."

The grandmother looked anxious and shook her head. "I don't like it, I don't like it." When she was excited she always said things twice over.

They went home slowly. On the way over the Weidendammer Bridge, Pony asked, "Grandmother, would you like to sit on the handlebars?"

"Stop such silly talk."

"Why? You aren't a bit heavier than Arthur Zickler, and he often sits there when I ride."

"If that happens just once again your father will take your bike away for good."

"Oh dear, I can't tell you a thing," scolded Pony.

When they came to the Heimbolds' house, 15 Schumann Street, there was great excitement. Everyone wanted to know where Emil was, and nobody knew.

The father suggested telegraphing Emil's mother.

"For heaven's sake!" cried his wife, Pony's mother. "She'd be frightened to death. About eight o'clock we'll all go to the station again. Perhaps he'll come on the next train."

"I hope so," mourned the grandmother, "but I can't help feeling — I don't like it. I don't like it."

"I don't like it," said Pony Hütchen, and thoughtfully wagged her small head to and fro.

Eighth Chapter

The Boy with the Auto Horn Turns Up

AT TRAUTENAU STREET, on the corner of Kaiser Avenue, the man with the stiff hat got off the car. Emil saw him, took up his bag and his bouquet, and said to the man reading the paper, "Thank you again and again, sir," and climbed off the platform.

The thief went in front of the car, crossed the tracks, and headed for the other side of the street. The car went on, and when the way was clear Emil noticed that the man stopped, hesitated a moment, and then walked up the steps to an outdoor café.

Now again it was necessary to be very cautious. Like a detective that follows a clue, Emil sized up the situation, looked quickly around, noticed a newsstand on a corner, and ran as fast as he could to hide behind it.

His hiding place was perfect. It lay between the stand and a post. The boy put down his baggage, took off his cap, and peeked out.

The man had seated himself on the terrace close to the railing. He was smoking a cigarette and seemed very pleased with himself. Emil was disgusted that a thief could be so thoroughly satisfied while the fellow who was robbed had to be so gloomy and not know what to do.

What a silly idea to hide behind a newsstand as if he himself were the thief instead of the other. What point was there in knowing that the man was sitting in Café Josty on Kaiser Avenue and that he was drinking light beer and smoking cigarettes? If the fellow would get up, then the chase could go on. But if he stayed there then Emil might hide behind the stand until he grew a long gray beard. Nothing was wanting now but for a policeman to come along and say, "My son, you look suspicious. Come, follow me of your own accord, now, or I'll have to put the handcuffs on you."

Suddenly a horn tooted right behind Emil. He jumped aside in fright and turned around to see a boy who stood there laughing at him.

"There man, don't get excited," said the boy.

"Who honked that horn behind me?" asked Emil.

"Why me of course. You don't come from Wilmersdorf, do you? Otherwise you'd have known long ago that I have a horn in my pants' pocket. Everyone around here knows me as well as if I were a freak."

"I'm from Neustadt. I just came from the station."

"From Neustadt, eh? That's why you've got such a goofy suit on?"

"Take that back! Or I'll give you one that'll lay you out cold."

"Shucks, man," said the other cheerfully, "are you cross? The weather's too excellent for fighting, but it's O.K. with me."

"We'll tend to that later," declared Emil. "I haven't any time for such stuff now." And he looked across at the café to see if Grundeis was still sitting there.

"I thought you had all the time in the world. Get behind a newsstand with his bag and his flowers and then start to play hide-and-go-seek with himself. A fellow must have ten or twenty yards of time left over to do that."

"No," said Emil, "I'm watching a thief!"

"What? Did I understand the first time?" said the other. "Who did he swipe from?"

"Me!" answered Emil, and was positively proud of it. "In the train. While I was asleep. A hundred and forty marks. I was supposed to give them to my grandmother here in Berlin. Then he sneaked into another compartment and got out at the Zoo Station. Me after him, of course, you can imagine. Then on the streetcar. And now he's sitting over there in that café, with his stiff hat, patting himself on the back."

"But man, that is marvelous," cried the newcomer. "Just like a movie! And what are you going to do now?"

"No idea. Keep after him. That's all I know right now."

"Tell it to the cop there. He'll nab him for you."

"I don't dare. I pulled a stunt home in Neustadt — not so good — and they're after me now. And if I——"

"I get you."

"And my grandmother is waiting at the Friedrich-strasse Station."

The boy with the horn thought a bit. Then he said, "This looks like a swell stunt to me — some class, I'll say. And man, I'm with you, if it's all right with you."

"That would be mighty good of you."

"Oh, cut it out, boy. One thing's sure. I'm in on it. My name's Gustav."

"And mine's Emil."

They shook hands, well pleased with each other.

"But let's get going," advised Gustav. "If we do nothing but stand around here the crook will give us the slip. Have you any money?"

"Not a cent."

Gustav honked softly to stir up his thoughts. It didn't help.

"How would it be," asked Emil, "if you got a few of your friends to help?"

"Man, the idea is superb," cried Gustav excitedly. "All I have to do is to dash through the courtyards honking, and we'll have the whole outfit."

"Do it, then, but come back soon," Emil advised him, "or else that thief over there will run away. And me after him, of course. And when you get back I'll be out of sight."

"True enough. I'll hurry! Count on that. Anyhow, the bozo in the Café Josty there is eating boiled eggs and such things. He'll stay a while. So see you later, Emil. Man, I'm crazy about it. This will be a humdinger." And with that he tore off.

Emil felt wonderfully relieved. Of course, bad luck is always bad luck. But to have a few supporters who are on your side of their own free will is no small comfort.

He kept close watch on the thief, who was doing himself rather well, probably on Emil's mother's savings, too, and Emil had only one anxiety — that the man might get up and leave. Then Gustav and his horn and everything else would be of no use.

But Herr Grundeis did him the favor of staying where he was. If he'd had any idea of the conspiracy that was drawing around him like a bag he would have hired an airplane, at least. For now things were getting hot for him.

Ten minutes later Emil heard the horn again. He

turned and saw at least two dozen boys marching down Trautenau Street with Gustav in the lead.

"Everybody halt! There, what do you say?" asked Gustav, his face all smiles.

"It's great," answered Emil, and poked Gustav in the ribs in his joy.

"Now, gentlemen, this is Emil from Neustadt. I've already told you the rest. Over across there sits the pig dog who swiped his money. That one to the right on the balcony with the black melon on his bean. If we let that brother get away our name is Mud from then on. Understand?"

"But Gustav, we'll get him all right," said a boy with horn spectacles.

"That is the Professor," explained Gustav.

And Emil shook hands with him.

Then the whole gang was introduced, one after the other.

"There," said the Professor, "now we'll step on the gas. Let's go! First, the money!"

Everyone gave what he had. The pieces clinked into Emil's cap. There was even one whole mark piece there. It came from a very small boy named Dienstag. He was so excited that he hopped from one foot to the other, and he was allowed to count the money.

"Our capital amounts to five marks and seventy pfennig," he announced to his eager listeners. "The

"There, what do you say?" asked Gustav, his face all smiles.

best thing to do would be to divide the money between three people, in case we have to separate."

"Good," said the Professor. He and Emil took two marks apiece. Gustav got one mark, seventy pfennig.

"Thank you ever so much," said Emil. "As soon as we get him I'll pay you back. What do we do now? First I'd rather take my bag and my flowers some place. Because when the chase begins they'll be terribly in my way."

"Man, give me the stuff," demanded Gustav. "I'll take it right over to the Café Josty, leave it at the counter, and have a look at Mr. Thief at the same time."

"But watch your step," called the Professor. "The crook need not know that there are detectives on his trail. That would make it harder to get him."

"Do you think I'm loony?" grumbled Gustav and started off.

"A fierce face for the pictures, the man has," he remarked when he returned. "And the things are well taken care of. We can get them when we want them."

"Now it would be best for us to hold a council of war," advised Emil. "But not here. It might be noticed."

"We'll go to Nikolsburger Place," decided the Professor. "Two of us will stay here at the newsstand and watch to see that the fellow doesn't beat it. We'll appoint five or six as scouts, who will relay the news. Then we'll come back on the hotfoot."

"Leave it to me," called Gustav, and began immediately to organize his intelligence men. "I will stay here with the scouts," he said to Emil, "don't worry. We won't let him get away. And you fellows speed up a little. It's a few minutes past seven already. All set, now, and step on it."

He appointed the scouts. And the others, with Emil and the Professor in the lead, streamed off to Nikolsburger Place.

Ninth Chapter

The Detectives Assemble

THEY SEATED THEMSELVES on two white benches
that stood on the grounds and on the low iron
railing surrounding the grassplot and looked solemn.
The boy who was called the Professor had apparently
been waiting for this day. He took off his spectacles and
waved them around as his father, the Judge, did as he
sketched out his program. "There is the possibility,"
he announced, "that we will have to separate, for prac-
tical reasons. Therefore we must have a central telephone station. Which of you has a telephone?"

Twelve boys spoke up.

"And which one of you that owns a telephone has
the most sensible parents?"

"I guess I have," sang out Dienstag.

"Your telephone number?"

"Bavaria 0579."

"Here are pencil and paper. Krummbiegel, make twenty slips and write Dienstag's telephone number on each one. But write clearly. And then give each one of us a slip. The telephone central must always know where the detectives are and what's going on. And whoever wants to get in touch will just call up little Dienstag and get accurate information from him."

"But I won't be at home," said little Dienstag.

"Yes indeed, you will be at home," retorted the Professor. "As soon as we are through with this conference you will go home and attend to the telephone."

"But I'd much rather be around when the criminal is caught. Little boys like me can be very useful at such times."

"You go home and stay by the telephone. That's a very responsible position."

"Well, all right, if you want me to."

Krummbiegel distributed the slips of paper. And each boy put his away carefully in his pocket. Several of the most thorough learned the number by heart at once.

"We ought to have some sort of reserves, too," suggested Emil.

"Of course. All who aren't absolutely needed in the hunt stay here in Nikolsburger Place. You'll take turns in going home to tell them that probably you'll be very late in coming home tonight. Some of you might say that you are spending the night with a friend — so that we will have substitutes and reserves if the chase lasts till morning. Gustav, Krummbiegel, Arnold, Mittenzwey, his brother, and I will call up in the meanwhile that we are staying out. Yes, and Traugott will go along to the Dienstags' as messenger and will run to Nikolsburger Place if we need anyone. Then we'll have the detectives, the reserves, the telephone bureau, and the messengers. Those are the most necessary departments, for the time being."

"We will need something to eat," suggested Emil. "Perhaps a few of you could go home and bring back some sandwiches."

"Who lives nearest?" asked the Professor. "Off with you, Mittenzwey, Gerold, Friedrich the First, Brunot, Zerlett. Scoot and bring back some eats."

The five boys darted off.

"You blockheads, you rattle on all the time about eating and telephones and sleeping out. But how you're going to catch your man — that you don't ever mention. You — you — school — schoolteachers," growled Traugott. He couldn't think of a deeper insult.

"Have you a machine for taking fingerprints?" asked Petzold.

"Perhaps, if he was very sly, he wore rubber gloves. And if so there would be nothing you could prove against him." Petzold has been to twenty-two detective-story movies, and you can see they had done him no good.

"You're simply moth-eaten," said Traugott, disgusted. "They will just wait for the chance and take back from him the money he swiped."

"Nonsense," objected the Professor, "if we steal money from him, we'll be the same sort of thieves that he is."

"Don't be funny," cried Traugott. "If somebody steals from me and I steal back I'm no thief."

"Yes, you are too a thief," the Professor decided.

"Applesauce," murmured Traugott.

"The Professor is right," Emil broke in. "If I take anything from anybody secretly then I am a thief. And it is all the same whether it belonged to him or whether he had just stolen it from me."

"That's exactly right," said the Professor. "But please do me the favor of not making wise speeches here that don't do any good. The business is all arranged. How we are going to get the crook we can't tell yet. That we must plan out as we go along. One thing is sure — that he must give back the money of his own free will. To steal it would be idiotic."

"That I don't understand," objected the little Dienstag. "I can't steal what belongs to me! What's mine is mine, even if it is sticking in someone else's pocket."

"Those are differences that are hard to understand," expounded the Professor. "Morally, you are right, in my opinion, but the Court will decide against you, just the same. Even many grownups do not understand it, but it is so."

"It's all the same to me," said Traugott, and shrugged his shoulders.

"And look sharp, now, can you act like a sleuth?" asked Petzold. "Otherwise he'll turn around and see you, and then goodnight!"

"Yes, it will take good sleuthing," agreed little Dienstag. "That's why I thought you could use me. I can sneak along wonderfully. And I would be a whiz as a kind of police dog. I can bark, too."

"Yes, sneak along in Berlin so that no one will see you," Emil was irritated. "If you want everyone to look at you just begin to sneak along."

"But you must have a revolver," cried Petzold. He wasn't to be squelched for his suggestions.

"You do need a revolver," agreed two or three others.

"No," said the Professor.

"The thief surely has one." Traugott wanted to bet on it.

"This business is dangerous," declared Emil, "and anyone who is afraid had better go home to bed."

"Do you mean to say that I'm a coward?" inquired Traugott fiercely as he strode to the center like a professional boxer.

"Order," called the Professor, "thrash that out to-

morrow. What sort of a performance is that? You behave just like — like children!"

"But that's just what we are," said little Dienstag,
and everybody had to laugh.

"I really ought to write my grandmother a note,"
said Emil, "because my relatives have no idea where I
am. They might even run to the police. Could anyone
take a letter for me while we are chasing the fellow?
They live at 15 Schumann Street. That would be very
kind!"

"Let me," said a boy whose name was Bleuer. "But
write quickly, so that I can get there before the house
is closed. I'll go as far as the Oranienburger Gate on
the subway. Who will stake me?"

The Professor gave him money for the fare. Twenty
pennies for going and coming. Emil borrowed pencil
and paper and wrote:

Dear Grandmother:
   You must be worrying about where I am. I am in Berlin.
But I'm sorry I can't come right now because I have to
attend to some important business first. Don't ask about it.
And don't worry. When everything is settled, I'll be glad
to come along. The boy with the letter is a friend and
knows where I am. But he can't tell you. Because it is an
official secret. Love to Uncle, Aunt, and Pony Hütchen.
   Your faithful grandson,   EMIL
   P.S. Mother sent her love. I have flowers for you, too.
You'll get them as soon as I bring them.

Then Emil wrote the address on the other side,

folded the paper together, and said, "But don't you tell any of my family where I am and that the money is gone, or I'll be in hot water."

"O.K. Emil," said Bleuer. "Give me the telegram. When I come back I'll ring little Dienstag to hear what has happened meanwhile. And count me in on the reserve staff." Then he hurried off.

Meanwhile the five boys had returned with packages of sandwiches. Gerold even brought along a whole sausage. He had got it from his mother, he said. Well, maybe.

The five had informed their families that they would be away for a few hours more. Emil divided the sandwiches, and each put one away in reserve in his pocket. Emil kept the sausage under his own care.

Then five other boys ran home to see if they, too, might stay away a while longer. Two of them did not return. Apparently their parents forbade it.

The Professor gave the password, so that they might always know, if anyone came or telephoned, whether he was one of them. The password was "Emil." That was easy to understand.

Then little Dienstag, with Traugott, the grumbling messenger, went off, saying, "Well, hope you choke, boys." The Professor called after him to go to his house and tell his father that he had important business to attend to. "Then he'll be relieved and have nothing against it," he added.

"My word!" said Emil, "but there are splendid parents in Berlin."

"Don't imagine that they are all so nice," said Krummbiegel, and scratched himself behind his ears.

"Oh well, the average one is all right," answered the Professor. "It is the most sensible way to be. This way we don't lie to them. I've promised my parents not to do anything that's wrong or dangerous. And as long as I keep my word, I can do what I want to. He is a splendid fellow, my father."

"Simply great!" repeated Emil. "But listen, perhaps it will be dangerous today."

"Well, then, it's off with the permission," admitted the Professor and shrugged his shoulders. "He said that I should always see to it that I behave just as if he were with me. And I'm doing that today. So now we'll cut off."

He planted himself before the band and called out, "The detectives expect you to do your duty. The telephone central is established. I'll leave my money with you. There is still a mark, fifty pennies. Here, Gerold, take it and count it. Provisions are here. Money we have. Everybody knows the telephone number. One more thing: whoever has to go home, beat it. But at least five people must stay. Gerold, you must be responsible for that. Show that you are real boys. Meanwhile we'll do our best. When we need substitutes little

Dienstag will send Traugott to us. Has anyone another question? Is everything clear? Password, Emil!"

"Password, Emil!" shouted the boys so that Nikolsburger Place shook, and the passers-by looked daggers.

Emil was almost happy that his money had been stolen from him.

Tenth Chapter

A Taxi Is Trailed

THREE OF THE STAFF RUNNERS came storming out of Trautenau Street, brandishing their arms about wildly.

"Off!" said the Professor, and on the second he, Emil, the Mittenzwey boys, and Krummbiegel ran toward Kaiser Avenue as if they were trying to break the record for the hundred-yard dash. The last twelve yards to the newsstand they took very carefully, and held back, because Gustav motioned to them to stop.

"Too late?" asked Emil out of breath.

"Are you crazy, man?" whispered Gustav. "When I do anything I do it right."

The thief was standing across the street in front of the Café Josty, looking around at the view as if he were in Switzerland. Presently he bought an evening paper from the newsboy and began to read.

"If he comes across and runs into us now," murmured Krummbiegel, "it will be a nasty business."

They stood behind the newsstand, craning their necks around the side, and trembled with excitement.

The thief took not the slightest notice, but turned the pages of his paper with admirable perserverance.

"He must be squinting over the edge, though, to see if anyone is spying on him," Mittenzwey the older decided.

"Has he looked over toward you often?" asked the Professor.

"Not a blink. He gobbled as if he hadn't eaten for three days."

"Attention!" called Emil.

The man in the stiff hat folded up his paper, glanced over the passers-by, and then like lightning beckoned to an empty taxi that was passing. The taxi stopped, the man got in, and the taxi rolled off.

But presto, there sat the boys in another taxi, and Gustav was saying to the driver: "Do you see that car that's just turning into Prager Place? Yes? Drive behind it, please. But be careful, so that he won't notice." The car started up, crossed Kaiser Avenue, and traveled along at a safe distance behind the other taxi.

"What's up?" asked the chauffeur.

"The fellow ahead there pulled a raw one, and we're

sticking to him like burrs," explained Gustav. "But that's just between ourselves, understand?"

"Just as you gentlemen wish," answered the chauffeur, and inquired further: "But have you any money?"

"What do you take us for?" called the Professor reproachfully.

"Oh well," grumbled the man.

"I A. 3733 is his number," Emil informed them.

"That's important," decided the Professor, and made a note of the figures.

"Not too near to the fellow," warned Krummbiegel.

"All right," mumbled the chauffeur.

So they went down Motz Street, down Viktoria-Luise Place and on down Motz Street again. Some people stopped on the sidewalk and laughed at the strange company of gentlemen in the taxi.

"Duck," whispered Gustav. The boys threw themselves on the floor of the cab and lay huddled together like cabbages and turnips.

"What's the matter?" asked the Professor.

"There's a red light at Luther Street, man! You've got to stop there, and the other car won't get across, either."

Sure enough, both cars stopped and waited, one behind the other, until the green light came on and gave the right of way again. But no one could have told that the second car was occupied. It seemed empty. The boys crouched down to give it that appearance. The chauffeur turned around, saw the performance, and had to laugh. As the car drove on they all bobbed up cautiously again.

"If only the trip doesn't last too long," said the Professor, as he inspected the meter. "This joy ride has cost eighty pfennigs already."

The journey was even then coming to an end. At Nollendorf Place the first taxi stopped right in front of the Hotel Kreid. The second car put on its brakes at the same moment and waited outside the danger zone for whatever might happen next.

The man in the stiff hat got out, paid his fare, and disappeared into the hotel.

"Gustav, after him!" commanded the Professor anxiously. "If that place has two entrances he is off." Gustav vanished.

Then the other boys got out. Emil paid. It cost one mark. The Professor led his followers through a gate leading past a movie theater into a great courtyard that stretched behind the theater to Nollendorf Place. Then he sent Krummbiegel out to catch Gustav.

"Lucky for me if the guy stays in the hotel," decided Emil. "This courtyard makes a wonderful headquarters."

"With all the modern conveniences," added the Professor, "subway station over there, telephone booths, and places to hide. It couldn't be better."

"Hope Gustav will get out of it all right," said Emil.

"Trust him," answered Mittenzwey the younger. "He's not as dumb as he looks."

"If only he'd come soon," worried the Professor, and seated himself in a chair that had been left in the courtyard. He looked like Napoleon before the Battle of Leipzig.

And then Gustav came back.

"We've got him!" he said, and rubbed his hands together. "He is really staying in the hotel. I saw the elevator boy take him upstairs. There isn't any other entrance, either. I looked the joint over from all sides. If he doesn't go off over the roof, he is trapped."

"Krummbiegel is keeping watch?" asked the Professor.

"Of course, man!"

Then Mittenzwey the elder got a nickel, ran into a café, and telephoned little Dienstag.

"Hello! Dienstag?"

"Yes, speaking," crowed little Dienstag at the other end.

"Password, Emil. This is Mittenzwey, senior. The man in the stiff hat is staying at Hotel Kreid in Nollendorf Place. The headquarters is located in the courtyard of the West movie, the left entrance."

Little Dienstag noted it all down conscientiously, repeated it, and then asked, "Do you need any reinforcements, Mittenzwey?"

"No!"

Little Dienstag noted it all down conscientiously.

"Was it hard up to now?"

"Oh, so so. The guy took a taxi, and we took another, you understand, and kept right behind him until he got out. He's taken a room and is up there now. Probably looking to see who's under the bed and playing skat with himself."

"What's the room number?"

"We don't know yet. But we'll get it soon."

"How I wish I were there with you! Do you know, the first time after vacation that we can choose our own theme subjects I'm going to write it up."

"Any of the others called up yet?"

"No, no one. It makes me sick."

"Well, so long, little Dienstag."

"Success to you, gentlemen. What else did I want to say? . . . Password, Emil!"

"Password, Emil," replied Mittenzwey, and reported back to headquarters in the courtyard of the West movie. It was already eight o'clock. The Professor went to check up on the guard.

"We won't get him today, that's sure," said Gustav fretfully.

"Still, it will be lucky for us if he goes right to bed," Emil explained. "For if he runs around for hours more in an auto and goes to restaurants, or to dance, or to the theater, or all together, we'll have to dig up a little foreign credit beforehand."

The Professor came back, sent the two Mittenzweys

as communication men to Nollendorf Place, and was very preoccupied. "We must plan some way to keep a closer watch on the man," he said. "Everybody think hard, please."

So they all sat for a long time and pondered heavily.

Just then a bell tinkled through the yard, and into the court rolled a small nickel-plated bicycle. Seated upon it was a small girl, and doing the pedaling was Comrade Bleuer. They both sang out, "Hurrah!"

Emil jumped up, helped them both off the bike, shook hand enthusiastically with the little girl, and announced to the others, "This is my cousin, Pony Hütchen."

The Professor politely offered his chair to Pony, and she seated herself.

"There now Emil, you villain," she said. "Come to Berlin and immediately act like a movie. We were just going back to the Friedrichstrasse Station to meet the next train for Neustadt when your friend Bleuer came with the note. A nice boy, too. Congratulations."

Bleuer stuck out his chest and blushed.

"Now then," continued Pony. "Mother and Father and Grandmother are waiting at home, having brainstorms trying to figure out what really is the matter with you. Of course, we didn't tell them anything. I just stopped Bleuer in front of the house and skipped off a little while. But I must go right back home, or else they'll be calling the police. Because another child

99

lost on the self-same day — that would be more than their nerves could stand."

"Here is the groschen* for the return trip," said Bleuer, very proud. "We saved it." The Professor put the money away.

"Were they cross?" asked Emil.

"Not a bit," answered Pony. "Grandmother galloped around the room crying, 'Grandson Emil has just gone to make a call on the President,' until Mother and Father quieted her down. But you'll have the guy by tomorrow, I hope? Who is your Sherlock Holmes?"

"Here," said Emil, "that is the Professor."

"So pleased, Professor," declared Pony, "to meet a real detective at last."

The Professor laughed sheepishly and stuttered a few unintelligible words.

"And now," said Pony, "here is my pocket money — fifty-five pfennigs. Buy yourself some cigars."

Emil took the money. Pony sat like the queen of beauty on her throne, and the boys stood around her like the judges.

"And now I must make myself scarce," said Pony Hütchen. "I'll be here early tomorrow. Where are you going to sleep? Gee, but I'd like to stay here and make your coffee in the morning. But what can you do? A woman's place is in the home. So long. See you later, gentlemen. Good night, Emil!"

---

* A ten-pfennig piece.

She gave Emil a clap on the shoulder, jumped on her bike, tinkled the bell gaily, and rolled away.

The detectives stood for some time, speechless.

Finally the Professor opened his mouth and said, "Great gosh!"

And the others agreed heartily.

Eleventh Chapter

A Spy Slips into
the Hotel

TIME PASSED SLOWLY. Emil visited the three out-
posts and wanted to relieve one of them. But
Krummbiegel and the two Mittenzweys announced
that they were staying. Whereupon Emil ventured
very cautiously to the Hotel Kreid, picked up the
latest bulletins, and returned to the courtyard in great
excitment.

"I have the feeling," he said, "that something must
be done. We can't leave the hotel all night without anyone to watch. To be sure, Krummbiegel is standing at
the corner of Kleist Street. But he only has to turn his
head, and Grundeis can go flying off in the other
direction."

"That is all very well," returned Gustav. "But we

can't just run to the porter and say, 'Listen, we're just going to sit here on these steps.' And you yourself certainly can't go into the building. If the guy should poke his head out of his door and recognize you, the whole performance so far would be no good."

"That isn't what I meant," answered Emil.

"What then?"

"Well, there's a boy in the hotel. The one who runs the elevator and such. If one of us should go to him and tell him what's up — he knows the hotel like his own vest pocket. He'll surely have a good idea."

"Good," said the Professor, "that's fine." He had a comical habit of acting as though he were giving out marks to the others. That was why he was called the Professor.

"This Emil — another hunch like that, and we'll make him the mayor. As smart as a Berliner," cried Gustav.

"Don't imagine that you're the only smart ones!" Emil was emphatic. He felt his pride in Neustadt wounded.

"Anyway, we still have a fight to finish."

"What for?" asked the Professor.

"Well, he made fun of my best suit."

"The fight can come off tomorrow," the Professor decided, "tomorrow or not at all."

"Oh, the suit isn't so bad. I'm getting used to it," Gustav declared good-naturedly. "But we can fight anyway. Only you might as well take notice that I am the champion of the gang. So watch out!"

"And in school I am the best of any weight," boasted Emil.

"It's terrible the way you brag of your muscles," said the Professor. "I'd really like to go over into the hotel myself. But I can't leave you two alone a minute, because you always start a fight."

"Then I'll go!" broke in Gustav.

"Right," said the Professor, "you go! And talk to the boy. But be careful! Perhaps something can be done. Find out for sure what room the fellow is in. In an hour come back and bring the information."

Gustav vanished.

The Professor and Emil packed back and forth before the door and talked to each other about their teachers. Then the Professor picked out the differences between the German and foreign license plates that went by until Emil understood a little about them. And then they thoughtfully ate a sandwich together.

By this time it was dark. Electric ads flamed everywhere. The elevated thundered overhead. The subway rumbled beneath. Streetcars and motorbuses, private cars and motorcycles, made a crazy concert. Dance music came from the Woerz Café. The movie theater on Nollendorf Place began its last show. And many people crowded in.

"Such a big tree as that over by the station looks like a freak here," mused Emil. "It looks as if it had lost its way." The boy was enchanted and thrilled. And he almost forgot why he was there and that he had lost a hundred and forty marks.

"Of course, Berlin is wonderful. You'd think you were sitting in a movie. But I'm not sure whether I'd want to live here always. In Neustadt we have an Upper Market and a Lower Market and a Station Square! And the playgrounds by the river and in Amsel Park. That is all. But still, Professor, I believe it is enough for me. Always such a holiday racket, always a hundred thousand streets and squares? I'd be lost all the time. Imagine if I didn't have you with me and were standing here all alone! It gives me the creeps to think of it."

"You get used to it," answered the Professor. "Probably I couldn't stand it in Neustadt, with its three squares and its Amsel Park."

"You get used to it," said Emil, "but Berlin is a great sight. No doubt of it, Professor. Wonderful."

"Is your mother really very strict?" asked the Berlin boy.

"My mother?" asked Emil. "Not a bit of it. She lets me do everything. But I don't. You understand?"

"No," the Professor said frankly, "I don't understand."

"No? Well, then, I'll tell you. Have your people much money?"

"I don't know about that. We don't talk much about it at home."

"I guess, when people don't talk much about it, it means they have plenty of it."

The Professor considered a moment and then admitted, "That is quite likely."

"You see. We often talk about it, my mother and I. We have very little. And she has to keep on earning, and still there's hardly ever enough to make both ends meet. But when we have a class excursion my mother gives me just as much money as any of the other boys get. Sometimes even more."

"How can she, though?"

"That I don't know. But she can. And then I bring half of it back."

"Does she want you to?"

"Silly! I want to!"

"Uhuh!" said the Professor. "That's the way it is."

"Yes, just like that. And if she lets me go out into the country with Prötzsch, who lives upstairs, and stay until nine o'clock, I come back by seven because I don't want her to sit in the kitchen and eat her supper alone. Of course she wanted me to stay with the others. And I tried it, too. But it wasn't any fun. Anyway inside she is glad that I come home early."

"Uhm," said the Professor, "it's entirely different at our house. If I really come home on time I can bet that they'll be at the theater or invited out somewhere. We like each other all right. I must say that. But we don't make any fuss about it."

"That is the only thing we can afford. But that doesn't make me a mamma's baby, not by a long shot. And if anybody doesn't believe that, I'll smash him against the wall. That's very simple to understand."

"I do understand."

The two boys stood for a while in the gateway without speaking. Night came. And the moon peeped with one eye over the elevated.

The Professor cleared his throat and asked without looking at the other, "You're pretty fond of each other, aren't you?"

"Frightfully," answered Emil.

Twelfth Chapter

A Green Elevator Boy
Bursts from His Cocoon

ABOUT TEN O'CLOCK a detachment of the guard appeared in the courtyard, brought along enough sandwiches to feed a hundred hungry men, and asked for further orders.

The Professor was much annoyed and explained that they had no business there at all, but should have waited at Nikolsburger Place for Traugott, the messenger from the telephone bureau.

"Don't get so mad!" said Petzold. "Naturally we are simply curious to know how things look here with you."

"And besides, we thought something had happened to you because Traugott never showed up," Gerold added apologetically.

"How many are there still at Nikolsburger Place?" asked Emil.

"Four. Or rather three," Friedrich the First corrected himself.

"There might even be only two," added Gerold.

"Don't ask them again," cried the Professor angrily, "or they'll say next that there's nobody there at all, now."

"For heaven's sake, don't shout so," said Petzold. "I don't give a hoot for being ordered around by you."

"I move that Petzold be thrown out at once and that he is forbidden to take any further part in the chase," stormed the Professor, and stamped his foot.

"I'm sorry that you two get mad at each other on my account," said Emil. "We ought to vote like the senate. I move that Petzold just be given strict warning. Because, naturally, it isn't possible for each one of us to do just what he wants."

"Think you're smart, don't you, you pigs. I'm going anyhow, if you want to know." Then Petzold added something terribly impolite and left.

"It was all his idea. Otherwise we certainly wouldn't have come here," Gerold told them. "And Zerlett stayed back in the Reserve headquarters."

"Not another word about Petzold," commanded the Professor, and already he was talking quite calmly again. He took a firm grip on himself. "Dismissed."

"And now what becomes of us?" questioned Friedrich the First.

"It would be best for you to wait until Gustav comes back from the hotel and makes a report," Emil proposed.

"Good," said the Professor. "Isn't that the bellboy, there?"

"Yes, there he is," agreed Emil.

In the gateway stood a boy in a green livery with a rakish green cap at just the right angle on his head. He waved to the others and slowly strolled nearer.

"He's got a swell uniform, by thunder," said Gerold enviously.

"Do you bring news of our spy Gustav?" called the Professor.

The boy was by this time quite close. He nodded and said, "Yes, indeed."

"All right, what's happened?" asked Emil eagerly.

Suddenly a horn tooted, and the green boy jumped around as if he'd lost his senses — laughing all the while.

"Emil, man!" he called, "but you are dumb!"

Of course, it wasn't the bellboy at all, but Gustav himself.

"You green rascal!" scolded Emil jokingly.

Then the others laughed too, until someone in one of the houses on the court opened a window and shouted, "Quiet, down there!"

"Magnificent!" said the Professor. "But quieter, gentlemen. Come here, Gustav, sit down and tell us all about it."

"Man, it's as good as a movie. It's enough to make a cat laugh. Well, then, listen! I slunk into the hotel, saw the bellboy standing around, and gave him the high sign. He came over to me, and I told him the whole story straight from A to Z. About Emil. And about us. And about the thief. And that he was staying at the hotel. And that we had to look sharp so that we could get the money off him again tomorrow.

" 'Fine!' said the boy. 'I have another uniform. You put it on and make a second bellboy.'

" 'But what will the head porter say about that? He'll surely tattle,' I answered.

" 'He won't tell on us — he'll let us,' he said, 'because the porter is my father.'

"What he told his old man, I don't know. Anyway, I got the uniform. I can sleep in one of the empty servants' rooms and even bring someone else with me. Now, what do you say?"

"In what room is the thief staying?" asked the Professor.

"A fellow can't ever get a rise out of you, can he?" said Gustav disgruntled. "Naturally, I have no work to do. I must keep out of the way. The boy guessed that the thief was rooming in Number 61. So I ran up to the third story and played spy. So as not to attract any attention, you understand. Waited behind banisters, and so on. After about half an hour, sure enough, the door of 61 opened. And who came bustling out? Our Mr. Thief. I had looked him over this afternoon. It was our man, all right. Little black mustache, ears that the moon could shine through, and a face that I wouldn't take as a gift. As he came down the hall I rolled out in front of his legs, stood at attention, and asked him, 'Are you looking for anything, sir?'

" 'No,' he said. 'I don't need anything. Or, wait a minute! You can tell the clerk to call me at eight o'clock sharp tomorrow morning. Room 61. Don't forget!'

" 'No, you can depend on it, sir,' I said, and pinched myself in the pants I was so excited. 'I won't forget. At eight o'clock sharp the telephone bell will ring in Room 61.' They call people by telephone. He nodded quietly and drifted back to his room."

"Excellent!" The Professor was tremendously pleased, and the others too.

"At eight o'clock he'll have a bodyguard waiting for him at the hotel. Then the chase will go on. And then he'll be trapped."

"He is just as good as settled now," called Gerold.

"Please omit flowers," said Gustav. "And now I'll chase off. I must put a letter in the box for Number 12. A ten-cent tip. It's a profitable job. The bellboy gets as much as ten marks a day. So he says! Now then,

112

about seven o'clock I'll get up and take care that this guy is waked on the dot. And then I'll come back here."

"Good boy, Gustav, I'm grateful to you," said Emil solemnly. "Now nothing more can happen. Tomorrow he'll be caught. And now we can all go to sleep in peace, can't we, Professor?"

"Certainly. Everybody digs out and goes to bed. And tomorrow morning, eight o'clock sharp, all those present be back here. Anybody who can drag out some money, do it. I'll call up little Dienstag now. He can round up the others as reserves when they call him in the morning. We may have to corral the man. You never can tell."

"I'll go with Gustav to sleep in the hotel," said Emil.

"Let's go, man! It will suit you right down to the ground. It's superb!"

"I'll telephone first," planned the Professor. "Then I'll go home too and send Zerlett home. Otherwise he'll wait till morning at Nikolsburger Place for further orders. Is everything clear?"

"Yes, indeed, Mr. Chief of Police," laughed Emil.

"Tomorrow, here in the court, at eight sharp," said Gerold.

"Bring a little money," reminded Friedrich the First.

They separated. First they all shook hands solemnly. Some marched home. Gustav and Emil went into the hotel. The Professor crossed over Nollendorf Place to telephone little Dienstag from the Café Hahnen.

And an hour later they were all asleep. Most of them in their beds. Two in a servant's room on the fourth floor of the Hotel Kreid.

And one at the telephone in his father's armchair. That was little Dienstag. He did not desert his post. Traugott had gone home. But little Dienstag didn't stir from the telephone. He huddled down in the cushions and slept and dreamed of four million telephone conversations.

At midnight his parents came home from the theater. They were surprised to find their son in the armchair.

His mother picked him up and carried him to bed. He cuddled down and murmured in his sleep. "Password, Emil!"

Thirteenth Chapter

Herr Grundeis Acquires a Guard of Honor

THE WINDOWS OF ROOM 61 overlooked Nollendorf Place. And next morning Herr Grundeis noticed, as he was combing his hair, that there seemed to be countless children wandering around there. At least two dozen small boys were playing football before the grassplot in the center of the square. Another group stood on Kleist Street. Children were standing by the entrance to the subway.

"Evidently a holiday," he grumbled as he put on his tie.

Meanwhile the Professor was holding a business meeting in the theater court and scolding like an English sparrow.

"Here I crack my brains day and night on how to

catch the man, and you blockheads meanwhile mobilize the whole of Berlin. Perhaps we need an audience? Maybe we're making a movie? If the fellow slips through our clutches it will be your fault, you gossiping old maids!"

The others stood patiently in a circle, but did not seem to feel any serious twinges of conscience. They were not worried, and Gerold said, "Don't get excited, Professor, we'll get the thief one way or another."

"Oh, get out, you silly nutcrackers! And see to it that the crowd doesn't spread itself all over the map and that it doesn't watch the hotel. Get that? Forward, march!"

The boys moved away, and only the detectives remained in the courtyard.

"I borrowed ten marks from the porter," Emil informed them. "If the man bolts we'll have money enough to follow him."

"Just send those children out there home again," advised Krummbiegel.

"And do you really think they'd go? If Nollendorf Place should burst, they'd stay!" said the Professor.

"Only one thing will help us," announced Emil. "We must change our plan. We can't surround Grundeis with secret spies — instead we must simply hunt him down. So that he'll notice it. From all sides and with all the children."

"I've already thought of that too," declared the Professor. "We had best change our tactics and drive him into a corner until he has to give himself up."

"Marvelous," shouted Gerold.

"He would much rather give the money back than have a hundred children running and shrieking around him for hours till the whole city turns out and the police grab him," decided Emil.

The others nodded wisely. Just then a bell sounded in the gateway, and Pony Hütchen rode beaming into the courtyard.

"Good morning, detectives," she called, jumped off her saddle, greeted Cousin Emil, the Professor, and the others, and then produced a little basket that she had tied to the handlebars. "I've brought you coffee," she crowed, "and a few buttered rolls. I even have a clean cup. Oh, the handle is off! Something always goes wrong!"

Now the boys had all had breakfast. Even Emil in the Hotel Kreid. But no one wanted to hurt the little girl's feelings. So they drank coffee and milk out of the cup without a handle and ate rolls as if they had had nothing for four weeks.

"Umm — that tastes wonderful!" called Krumm-biegel.

"And how crisp the rolls are!" mumbled the Professor, chewing loyally.

"Isn't that so?" asked Pony. "Yes, it is always a bit different when there is a woman in the house!"

"In the courtyard," corrected Gerold.

"How are things in Schumann Street?" asked Emil.

"All right, thanks. And a special message from Grandmother. You'd better come soon, or as a punishment you'll have to eat fish every day."

"Oh, the dickens," murmured Emil and made a face.

"Why, the dickens?" Mittenzwey the younger wanted to know. "Fish is good." Everybody looked at him with amazement, as it was his habit never to say a word. At that his face got fiery red, and he hid himself behind his big brother.

"Emil can't eat a bite of fish. If he tries it he has to leave the room," Pony Hütchen explained.

So they chatted and were all in a very good humor. The boys were especially polite. The Professor held Pony's bike. Krummbiegel went to wash out the thermos bottle and the cup. Mittenzwey, senior, folded up the lunch paper very carefully. Emil fastened the basket back on the handlebars. Gerold tested the tires to see if there was enough air in them. And Pony Hütchen hopped around the courtyard, sang a song to herself, and told them all sorts of things meanwhile.

"Wait!" she cried suddenly and halted on one foot. "I have to ask you something. Why are there so frightfully many children out on Nollendorf Place? It looks like a vacation camp."

"They are inquisitive. They have heard about our

criminal hunt. And now they want to be in on it," explained the Professor.

Just then Gustav came running toward the gate, honked loudly, and shouted, "Quick! He's coming!" Everybody tried to get out at once.

"Attention: listen," shouted the Professor. "We'll surround him on all sides. Children behind him, children before him, children, left and right! Is that clear? Further orders we'll give as we go. March out!"

They leaped, ran, and stumbled out of the gate. Pony Hütchen alone stayed behind, feeling a little bit offended. But then she swung herself onto her tiny nickel-plated bike, muttering like her own grandmother, "I don't like the looks of this! I don't like the looks of this," and followed after the boys.

The man in the stiff hat came to the hotel door, walked slowly down the steps, and turned right toward Kleist Street. The Professor, Emil, and Gustav hurried their messengers here and there among the various groups of children. And three minutes later Herr Grundeis was surrounded.

He looked about on all sides, utterly bewildered. The youngsters were talking, laughing, jostling one another, and keeping step with him. Many of them stared at the man until he became embarrassed and looked straight ahead again.

Ssst! a ball flew right by his head. He jumped and quickened his pace. But immediately the children walked just as much faster. He tried to turn off suddenly into a side street. But another troop of youngsters came streaming after him.

"Man, he has a face — as if he wanted to sneeze," called Gustav.

"Run a little ahead of me," advised Emil. "He ought not to recognize me yet. He'll be up against that soon enough."

Gustav threw back his shoulders and strode before Emil like a boxer who is so muscle-bound he can hardly move. Pony Hütchen rode alongside the procession and tinkled her bell happily.

The man in the stiff hat was noticeably nervous. He had a dark foreboding of what was coming to him, and he strode along with giant steps. But it was of no use. He could not escape his enemies.

Suddenly he stopped stock-still, as if nailed to the spot, turned around, and ran back down the street he had just come up. The assembled children turned too, and the order of march was continued in the opposite direction.

Then a small boy — it was Krummbiegel — ran across in front of the man so that he stumbled.

"What's the matter with you, you young jackanapes?" he shouted, "I am going to call the police at once."

"Oh yeh, please do!" jeered Krummbiegel. "We've been waiting for that a long time. Just call them up!"

Herr Grundeis had no idea of calling them — quite the contrary. The situation was growing more uncomfortable for him every minute. He began to have unmistakable fears, and he did not know which way to turn. Already people were looking out of all the windows. Already the shopgirls were running out in front of the shops with their customers and asking what was happening. If a policeman should come now it would be all up with him.

Then the thief had an inspiration. He noticed a branch of the Commercial and Private Bank. He broke through the chain of children, hurried up to the door, and disappeared.

The Professor sprang to the door and yelled, "Gustav and I follow him. Emil stays here meanwhile. When Gustav honks, things can start. Then Emil comes in with ten boys. Hunt for the right ones meanwhile, Emil. It's going to be a ticklish business."

Then Gustav and the Professor vanished through the door.

Emil's ears drummed with his heartbeats. Now the affair must be settled. He called Krummbiegel, Gerold, the Mittenzwey brothers, and a few others, and ordered that the rest should scatter.

The children retreated a few steps from the bank building, but not far. They would not miss on any account what was about to happen.

Pony Hütchen asked a boy to hold her bike and stepped up to Emil.

"Here I am," she said. "Head high. It's getting serious now. Goodness, I'm as nervous as a witch!"

"Do you think perhaps I'm not?" queried Emil.

Fourteenth Chapter

Pins Have Their Good Points Too

WHEN GUSTAV AND THE PROFESSOR entered the bank, the man in the stiff hat was already standing at a cage on which was a sign, "Paying and Receiving Teller." He was waiting impatiently for his turn to come. The bank clerk was telephoning.

The Professor took up his stand near the thief and watched like a hunting dog. Gustav stood behind the man and had his hand in his pocket all ready to honk his horn.

Then the cashier came to the window and asked the Professor what he wanted.

"Thank you," he said, "this gentleman was here before me."

"What do you wish?" the cashier asked Herr Grundeis.

"Will you please change a hundred-mark note for two fifties and give me forty marks in silver," asked the latter as he reached into his pocket and laid a hundred-mark note and two twenties on the counter.

The cashier took the three notes and turned with them to his cash drawer.

"One moment!" cried the Professor loudly. "That money is stolen!"

"Whaaat?" asked the bank clerk, astonished, and turned about. His colleagues who occupied other offices, working at their mental arithmetic, stopped working and poked up their heads as if a snake had bitten them.

"That money does not belong to this man at all. He stole it from a friend of mine, and now he wants to change it so that no one can prove it," declared the Professor.

"Such impudence I've never met in all my whole life," said Herr Grundeis. Then he turned back to the cashier: "Pardon me!" and gave the Professor a ringing box on the ear.

"That will not change the affair in the least," declared the Professor, as he gave Grundeis in return such a sound punch that the man had to hang onto the counter. And now Gustav honked three times, frightfully loud. The bank clerks all jumped up, consumed with curiosity, and ran to the cashier's cage. The vice-president, head of the deposit department, came storming out of his office.

And through the door came ten boys on the run, Emil in the lead, and surrounded the man with the stiff hat.

"What in thunderation is the matter with the young imps?" cried the vice-president.

"The young imps think that I stole from one of them the money that I just gave to your cashier to change for me," answered Herr Grundeis, trembling with rage.

"That's just what it is!" called Emil, and sprang up to the cage. "A hundred-mark note and two twenty-mark notes he stole from me. Yesterday afternoon. On the train from Neustadt to Berlin. While I was asleep!"

"Can you prove that?" asked the cashier sternly.

"I have been in Berlin for a week, and yesterday was in the city from morning till night," said the thief, and laughed politely.

"What a dirty lie!" shouted Emil, and almost wept with rage.

"Can you prove that this is the man who sat with you in the train?" asked the vice-president.

"Of course he can't do that," said the thief carelessly.

"Because if you say you were alone with him on the train, then you have no witnesses," remarked one of the onlookers. And Emil's comrades looked worried.

"No!" cried Emil. "No, I have too a witness. It's Frau Jakob from Gross-Grünau. She sat in the compartment at first and got out later. And she told me to take her very best regards to Herr Kurzhals in Neustadt."

"It looks as though you'd have to produce an alibi," said the head of the deposit department to the thief. "Can you do that?"

"Naturally," he declared. "I live over at the Hotel Kreid —"

"But only since last night," cried Gustav. "I got myself in there as elevator boy, and I know, man!"

The bank clerks smiled at that and began to be more interested in the boys.

"For the present we had best keep the money here, Herr —" said the vice-president, and tore off a memorandum slip on which to write his name and address.

"Grundeis is his name!" called Emil.

The man in the stiff hat laughed out loud and said, "There, you see there must be a mistake. My name is Müller."

"Oh, how well he lies! He told me in the train that his name was Grundeis," cried Emil, furious.

"Have you identification papers?" asked the cashier.

"Unfortunately, not with me," answered the thief. "But if you will just wait a minute I'll bring them over from the hotel."

"The fellow is just lying. And it is my money. And I must have it back," cried Emil.

"But even if that's true, my boy," explained the cashier, "it isn't as simple as all that. How can you

126

prove that the money is yours? Is your name on it, perhaps? Or did you write down the numbers on the notes?"

"Of course not," said Emil. "Who thinks that he's going to be robbed? But anyway, it is my money, do you hear? And my mother gave it to me for my grandmother, who lives here at 15 Schumann Street."

"Was there a corner torn on one of the notes, or something else that wasn't just as usual?"

"No, I don't know."

"Really, my good sirs, I declare, on my honor, the money is mine. I wouldn't rob small children, would I?" asked the thief.

"Wait!" shouted Emil, and suddenly he was so happy that he jumped for joy. "Wait! In the train I fastened the notes into my coat with a pin. So there must be pinholes in the notes."

The cashier held the notes up to the light. The others held their breath.

The thief took a step back. The vice-president drummed nervously on the counter.

"The boy is right," cried the cashier, pale with excitement. "There are actually pinholes in the notes."

"And here is the pin, besides," said Emil, and laid the pin proudly on the counter. "I pricked myself, too."

At that the thief turned like lightning, shoved the children right and left so that they fell over one another, ran across the room, tore open the door, and was off.

"After him!" shouted the vice-president.

Everybody ran for the door.

When they got to the street, they found the thief already hemmed in by at least twenty small boys. They held onto his legs. They hung on his arms. They pulled at his coat. He threshed around as if he were crazy, but the children did not loosen their hold.

And then came a policeman on the run, whom Pony Hütchen had brought with her little bicycle. And the vice-president asked him earnestly to arrest the man that was named Grundeis as well as Müller, as apparently he was a train thief.

The cashier asked for time off, took the money and the pin, and went with them. Well, it was a funny procession. The policeman, the bank clerk, the thief in the middle, and after them ninety or a hundred children! So they streamed to the station house.

Pony Hütchen rode near by on her little nickel-plated bike, waved to the elated Emil, and called, "Emil, my boy! I'll hurry home and tell them the whole story."

The boy nodded back and said, "I'll be home for lunch! Give them my love!"

Pony called again, "Do you know what you look like? Like a big school picnic!" Then she curved around the corner, ringing loudly.

Fifteenth Chapter

Emil Visits Police Headquarters

THE PROCESSION MARCHED to the nearest police station. The policeman informed a captain what had happened. Emil filled in the report. Then he had to tell them when and where he was born, who he was, and where he lived. And the captain wrote it all down. In ink.

"And what is your name?" he asked the thief.

"Herbert Kiessling," answered the rascal.

That made the boys — Emil, Gustav, and the Professor — laugh out loud. And the bank clerk, who had given over the hundred and forty marks to the captain, joined in with them.

"Man, what a slippery eel!" cried Gustav. "First he is Grundeis. Then he is Müller. Now he is Kiessling. Now I am just crazy to know who he really is!"

"Silence!" growled the captain. "We'll find that out too."

Herr Grundeis, Müller, Kiessling gave his temporary address as the Hotel Kreid. Then he gave the date of his birth and his home. Identification papers he had none.

"And where were you until yesterday?" questioned the captain.

"In Gross-Grünau," declared the thief.

"That is certainly lying again," called the Professor.

"Silence!" growled the captain. "We'll find that out too."

The bank clerk wondered whether he might leave. Then information about him was noted down. He patted Emil kindly on the shoulder and departed.

"Did you yesterday afternoon steal a hundred and forty marks from the schoolboy, Emil Tischbein, on the train coming from Neustadt to Berlin, Kiessling?" questioned the captain.

"Yes," said the thief gloomily. "I don't know how — it happened very suddenly. The boy was sleeping in the corner. And then the envelope fell out. And then I picked it up and just wanted to look to see what was inside. And as I had absolutely no money at the time ——"

"What a swindler," cried Emil. "I had the money pinned tight in my jacket pocket. It could not have fallen out."

"And he wasn't in such great need of it either, or he

wouldn't have had Emil's money untouched in his pocket. Meanwhile he had to pay for a taxi, boiled eggs, and beer," remarked the Professor.

"Silence!" growled the captain. "We'll find that out too."

And he wrote down everything that was told.

"Could you let me go now, Officer?" asked the thief, and squinted out of very politeness. "I've admitted the theft. And you know where I live. I have business in Berlin and would like to tend to a few errands."

"Don't make me laugh," said the captain sternly, and called the police headquarters to have them send the patrol over, because a railway thief had been arrested in his district.

"When do I get my money?" inquired Emil anxiously.

"At police headquarters," said the captain. "You will go right over, and there everything will be arranged."

"Emil, man!" whispered Gustav, "now you'll have to go to 'Alex'* in the Black Maria."

"Stuff and nonsense," said the captain. "Have you any money, Tischbein?"

"Yes, indeed," answered Emil. "The boys took up a collection yesterday. And the porter of Hotel Kreid lent me ten marks."

"Genuine detectives! Confounded rascals!" scowled the captain. But the scolding sounded very good-

---

* "Alex" is what they call police headquarters.

natured. "Well then, Tischbein, you take the subway to Alexander Place and announce yourself to Criminal Sergeant Lurje. Anything further you will soon find out. And you'll get your money back there."

"Could I first take the ten marks back to the porter?" Emil wanted to know.

"Of course."

In a few minutes the police van came. And Herr Grundeis Müller Kiessling had to climb in. The captain gave the policeman seated inside the written report and the hundred and forty marks. Also the pin. And then the Black Maria rumbled off. The boys who stood in the street jeered at the thief. But he paid no attention. Probably because he was too proud of having the privilege of riding in a private car.

Emil shook hands with the captain and thanked him.

Then the Professor informed the children who had waited before the station that Emil would get his money at "Alex," and the chase was over. The children streamed off home in great crowds. Only the intimate friends took Emil to the hotel and to the Nollendorf subway station. And he told them to telephone little Dienstag at noon, so he would know how everything had come out. And he hoped very much to see them again before he went back to Neustadt. And he thanked them all from the bottom of his heart for their help. And they'd get their money back too.

"If you dare to give our money back, you'll get it in

the neck, man!" cried Gustav. "And besides, we have to fight — on account of your funny suit."

"Oh, man!" said Emil, and grabbed Gustav and the Professor by the hand. "I feel so good. We'd better let the fight go. It would break my heart to knock you down for the count."

"You wouldn't succeed in that, even if you were in a bad humor, you fathead!" cried Gustav.

And then the three went to Alexander Place to police headquarters, and they had to go through many corridors and past countless rooms. And at last they found Criminal Sergeant Lurje. He was just eating breakfast. Emil introduced himself.

"Aha," said Herr Lurje, chewing busily. "Emil Stuhlbein, our youthful amateur detective. Already announced by telephone. The Commissioner awaits you. He wants to talk to you. Come with me now."

"Tischbein is my name," corrected Emil.

"Six of one and half a dozen of the other," said Herr Lurje, and took another bite of roll.

"We'll wait here for you," the Professor decided. And Gustav called after Emil, "Make it snappy. When I see anybody chewing, I always get hungry myself."

Herr Lurje walked through more halls — left, right, left again. Then he knocked on a door. A voice called, "Come in!" Lurje opened the door a crack and said, chewing, "The little detective is here, Commissioner, Emil Fischbein. You know."

"Tischbein is my name," Emil explained emphatically.

"Fine name, too," said Herr Lurje, and gave Emil a shove so that he tumbled into the room.

The Commissioner was a very nice man. Emil had to be seated in a comfortable armchair and tell the whole story, every bit, from the beginning. At the end the Commissioner said solemnly, "So, and now you'll get your money back."

"Thank goodness!" Emil took a long breath and put his money away. And most carefully.

"But don't let it get stolen again!"

"No! Impossible! I'll take it right to Grandmother."

"Right! I had almost forgotten. You must give me your Berlin address. Are you staying a few days?"

"I'd like to," said Emil. "I live at 15 Schumann Street with the Heimbolds. That's my uncle's name. My aunt's, too."

"It's wonderful how you children did it," commented the Commissioner as he stuck a big cigar into his mouth.

"The fellows worked wonderfully, that's true," cried Emil excitedly. "This Gustav with his horn, and the Professor, and little Dienstag, and Krummbiegel, and the Mittenzwey brothers — all of them, in fact. It was a pleasure to work with them. Especially the Professor. He is an ace!"

"Well, yes, you yourself are not exactly made of mush," remarked the man as he puffed out a cloud.

"What I'd like to ask, Herr Commissioner, what will they do to Grundeis, or whatever my thief is called?"

"We have taken him to the Identification Bureau. There he will be photographed. And his fingerprints taken. And after that we will compare the picture and the fingerprints with the photographs in our Rogues' Gallery."

"What is that?"

"There we have pictures of all the convicted criminals. And there we have the fingerprints, footprints, and such of the criminals that we haven't caught yet but that we are hunting. It might be possible that the man who stole from you had committed other thefts and burglaries before he helped himself to your money. Isn't that true?"

"That's so. I hadn't thought of that at all!"

"Just a moment," said the nice Commissioner as the telephone rang. "Yes, indeed . . . something interesting for you . . . come right up to my room," he spoke into the transmitter. Then he hung up and said, "Now a few men from the papers will be along to interview you."

"What is that?" asked Emil.

"Interviewing means asking questions."

"It can't be!" cried Emil. "Will I be in the paper, then?"

"Apparently," said the Commissioner. "When a schoolboy catches a thief, he becomes famous."

There came a knock, and four men walked into the room. The Commissioner shook hands with them and told them briefly about Emil's experience. The four men busily wrote it down.

"Wonderful," said one of the reporters at the end. "The country boy as detective."

"Perhaps you'll engage him for a plain-clothes man," advised another laughing.

"Why didn't you go right to a policeman and tell him all about it?" asked a third.

Emil was embarrassed. He thought of Policeman Jesche in Neustadt and of his dream. And his throat felt very dry.

"Well?" queried the Commissioner.

Emil shrugged his shoulders and said, "Well, all right! Because in Neustadt I had painted a red nose and a big mustache on the monument of the Grand Duke Karl. Please, arrest me, Herr Commissioner!"

Then the five men laughed instead of drawing long faces. And the Commissioner cried, "But Emil, we couldn't afford to put our best detective in jail."

"No? Truly? Oh, I am glad of that," said the boy, much relieved. Then he turned to one of the reporters and asked, "Don't you know me?"

"No," said the man.

"You paid for my ticket yesterday on Line 177 because I didn't have any money."

"Sure enough," exclaimed the man. "Now I remember. You wanted to know my address so that you could send back my money."

"Will you take it now?" asked Emil, and took ten pfennigs out of his trousers pocket.

"But, nonsense," answered the man. "You had even introduced yourself."

"Surely, I often do," explained the boy. "Emil Tischbein is my name."

"My name is Kästner," said the journalist, and they shook hands.

"Splendid," cried the Commissioner. "Old acquaintances."

"And now, Emil," said Herr Kästner, "will you come with me for a bit to the editor's office? First we'll go somewhere and have cake with whipped cream."

"Couldn't I invite you?" asked Emil.

"What a proud rascal!" The men were very much amused.

"No, you must let me pay," said Herr Kästner.

"I'd like to," answered Emil, "but the Professor and Gustav are waiting outside for me."

"Of course we'll take them with us," declared Herr Kästner.

The other journalists still had all kinds of questions

gave them an exact statement. And they
~~ notes again.

"Is the thief really a new one?" asked one of the men.

"I think not," answered the Commissioner. "Perhaps we are due for a great surprise. Call me up anyway in an hour, gentlemen, all of you."

Then they all departed. And Emil went with Herr Kästner back to Criminal Sergeant Lurje. He was still chewing and said, "Aha, the little Überbein!"

"Tischbein," said Emil.

Then Herr Kästner took a taxi for Emil, Gustav, and the Professor, and they went first to a pastry shop. On the way, Gustav honked. And they were delighted when Herr Kästner jumped. In the pastry shop the boys were very jolly. They ate cherry tart with lots of whipped cream and told whatever occurred to them.

They told about the council of war in Nikolsburger Place, about the taxi chase, about the night in the hotel, about Gustav as the bellboy, about the excitement in the bank. And at the end Herr Kästner said, "You are certainly three wonderful boys."

At that, they were very proud of themselves, and each ate another piece of cake.

After that, Gustav and the Professor climbed into a motorbus. Emil reminded them to call up little Dienstag in the afternoon, and then he went with Herr Kästner to the newspaper office.

The newspaper building was huge. It was almost as

The reporters had many questions to ask.

big as the police headquarters at Alexander Place. And in the corridors there was such a rushing and bustling that you might think there was an obstacle race going on.

They came to a room in which a pretty blond lady was sitting. And Herr Kästner walked up and down and dictated to the lady with the typewriter everything that Emil had told him. Every once in a while he would stop and ask Emil, "Is that right?" And when Emil nodded Herr Kästner would start dictating again.

Then he called up the Police Commissioner.

"What's that you say?" cried Kästner. "Well, if that isn't absurd. . . . I mustn't tell him anything about it yet? Soooo, that too? Well, I *am* glad. . . . Thank you very much! That will be a real scoop."

He hung up, looked at the boy as if he had never seen him before, and said, "Emil, come with me quick! We must have your picture taken."

"Good gracious!" said Emil, astonished. However, he submitted to everything, went up three stories higher with Herr Kästner, and entered a very bright room with many windows. First he combed his hair and then he had his picture taken.

Finally Herr Kästner took him into the composing room — there was a clatter, like that of a thousand typewriters — Herr Kästner gave a man the sheets that the lovely blond lady had typed and said that he'd be right back up because the stuff was very important, but first

140

he had to send the youngster back to his grandmother.

Then they took the elevator to the ground floor and walked out to the entrance. Herr Kästner beckoned to a taxi, seated Emil, gave money to the chauffeur, although the boy did not want him to, and said, "Take my young friend to Number 15 Schumann Street."

They shook hands heartily. And Herr Kästner added, "My compliments to your mother when you get home. She must be a very dear woman."

"Indeed she is," said Emil.

"One thing more," called Herr Kästner as the car started off, "read the paper this afternoon. You'll be surprised, young man."

Emil turned and waved. And Herr Kästner waved back.

And then the taxi swung round a corner.

Sixteenth Chapter

The Police Commissioner
Sends His Regards

THE AUTOMOBILE had already reached Unter den
Linden. Emil knocked three times on the window
back of the driver. The car stopped. And the boy asked,
"Are we almost there?"

"Sure," said the man.

"I'm sorry to make you trouble," said Emil, "but first
I must go to Kaiser Avenue. To the Café Josty. There
is a bouquet for my grandmother there. And my suitcase, too. Would you please be so kind?"

"What do you mean — kind? Have you some money
in case I haven't enough?"

"I have money, Driver. And I must have the flowers."

"All right," said the man, turned left, went through
the Brandenburger Gate, and down the green, shady

Zoological Gardens to Nollendorf Place. That place seemed to Emil much more harmless and friendly, now that everything had turned out all right. But anyway he reached carefully into his inside breast pocket. The money was there.

Then they went up Motz Street to the very end, turned right, and stopped before the Café Josty.

Emil climbed out, betook himself to the counter, asked the maid to please give him his bag and his flowers, got them, thanked her, climbed back into the car, and said, "There, Driver, now to Grandmother's."

They turned around, traveled the long way back, over the river Spree, through old streets with gray houses.

The boy would have liked to observe the neighborhood. But his things seemed bewitched. The suitcase kept toppling over. And if the suitcase stood still for a minute, then the wind seized the white paper around the flowers so that it rustled and tore. And Emil had to watch out to keep the bouquet from flying away.

At last the driver put on the brakes. The car stopped. It was Number 15 Schumann Street.

"Well, here we are," said Emil and got out. "Do I owe you any more money?"

"No, instead you get back thirty pfennigs."

"Is that so?" said Emil. "Get yourself a few cigars with it."

"I chew tobacco, my boy," said the driver, and went off.

Then Emil climbed to the third floor and rang the bell at the Heimbolds' door. There was a great cry behind the door. Then it was opened. And there stood Grandmother. She grabbed Emil by the collar, gave him a kiss on the left cheek and a clap on the right cheek at the same time, dragged him into the room by his hair, and cried, "Oh, you young rascal, oh you young rascal!"

"Fine stories we hear about you," Aunt Martha said, smiling as she gave him her hand. And Pony Hütchen offered him her elbows. She was wearing one of her mother's aprons and she squeaked, "Careful, my hands are wet. I'm washing dishes — we poor women!"

Then they all went together into the living room. Emil had to take the place of honor on the sofa. And his grandmother and Aunt Martha beamed upon him as if he were a very valuable painting of Titian's.

"Have you the loot?" asked Pony.

"Of course," said Emil, took the three notes out of his pocket, gave one hundred and twenty marks to his grandmother, and said, "Here, Grandmother, here is the money. And Mother sends her best love. And you mustn't blame her because she hasn't sent you anything these last months. Business wasn't so very good. And so this time she's sending you more than usual."

"Thank you, my dear," answered the old woman,

144

gave back a twenty-mark note, and said, "That is for you because you are such a fine detective."

"No, I can't take it. You see I still have twenty marks from Mother in my pocket."

"Emil, a boy must obey his grandmother. Put it in your pocket at once."

"No, I shan't take it."

"What a boy!" cried Pony. "Nobody'd have to ask me twice!"

"Oh no, I don't want it."

"Either you take it or I'll get the rheumatism, I'll be so angry," declared his grandmother.

"Quick, put the money away," said Aunt Martha, and poked the note into his pocket.

"Well, if you really want me to," stammered Emil. "Thank you, Grandmother."

"I am the one to be thankful," she answered, and smoothed back Emil's hair.

Then Emil handed over his bouquet of flowers. Pony brought a vase. But when the flowers were unwrapped, they didn't know whether to laugh or cry.

"Just dried vegetables!" said Pony Hütchen.

"They've had no water since yesterday afternoon," explained Emil ruefully. "It's no wonder. When Mother and I bought them yesterday at Stamnitzen's, they were perfectly fresh."

"I'm sure they were, I'm sure they were," said Grandmother as she put the wilted flowers in water.

"Perhaps they'll freshen up," comforted Aunt Martha. "There, and now we will have dinner. Your uncle won't be home until evening. Pony, set the table!"

"All right," said the little girl.

"Emil, what are we going to have?"

"No idea."

"What do you like best?"

"Macaroni with ham."

"Well then, you know what we are going to have."

It is true that Emil had eaten macaroni with ham just the day before. But in the first place one can stand eating his favorite dish almost every day. And in the second place it seemed to Emil as if at least a whole week had gone by since yesterday's dinner with his mother in Neustadt. And he dug into the macaroni as if he were Herr Grundeis Müller Kiessling himself.

After the meal, Emil and Pony ran down into the street for a while, as the boy wanted to try out Pony's little nickel-plated bike. Grandmother lay down on the sofa. And Aunt Martha baked an apple cake. Her apple cakes were famous in the whole family.

Emil rode through Schumann Street. And Pony ran after him, holding fast to the saddle. She maintained she had to, or her cousin would fly away. Then Emil had to get off, and she turned circles and threes and eights for him.

Suddenly a policeman appeared who carried a portfolio and inquired, "Children, do the Heimbolds live here in Number 15?"

"Yes, indeed," said Pony. "We're Heimbolds. One minute, Officer." She put her bike in the cellar.

"Is there something wrong?" wondered Emil. He couldn't help thinking of that plagued Jeschke.

"Quite the contrary. Are you the boy Emil Tischbein?"

"Yes, I am."

"Um, well, you can congratulate yourself!"

"Who has a birthday?" asked Pony, returning.

But the policeman told them nothing. Instead he climbed up the stairs. Aunt Martha led him into the living room. The grandmother awoke and got up, filled with curiosity. Emil and Pony stood by the table, much excited.

"It's this way," said the policeman as he opened the portfolio. "The thief that the schoolboy Emil Tischbein helped to catch early this morning has been identified as a bank robber from Hanover who has been wanted for four weeks. This thief had stolen a great deal of money. And our identification bureau has given him over for trial.

"Besides that, he has made a confession. They got back most of the money, which was sewed in the lining of his clothes. Nothing but thousand-mark notes."

"Holy cats!" said Pony Hütchen.

"The bank," continued the officer, "has been offering

a reward for the last two weeks to anyone who could trace the man.

"And as you," he turned to Emil, "have caught the man, you get the reward. The Police Commissioner sends his regards, and is happy to know that your ability can be rewarded in this way."

Emil made a bow.

Then the officer took a bundle of notes from his portfolio and counted them out on the table. Aunt Martha, who was watching closely, whispered, "A thousand marks!"

"Good gracious!" cried Pony. "I give up."

Grandmother signed a receipt. Then the policeman left. But before he went, Aunt Martha gave him a big glass of cherry brandy out of Uncle's cupboard.

Emil sat down beside his grandmother and could not say a word. The old woman put her arm around him and said, shaking her head, "It is just unbelievable! It is just unbelievable!"

Pony Hütchen jumped upon a chair, started to beat time as if she were leading a chorus, and sang, "Now we'll invite, now we'll invite, all the other boys for a party."

"Yes," said Emil, "that's all right. But first of all — probably now — what do you think? — Mother could come to Berlin too. . . ."

Seventeenth Chapter

Frau Tischbein
Is All Excited

THE NEXT MORNING Frau Wirth rang the doorbell of Frau Tischbein's home in Neustadt.

"Morning, Frau Tischbein," she said. "How are you?"

"Good morning, Frau Wirth. I'm so worried. My boy hasn't sent me a word. Every time the bell rings I think it is the postman. Shall I do your hair?"

"No, I only came over to bring you some news."

"Please . . ."

"Greetings from Emil and —— "

"For heaven's sake, what happened to him? Where is he? What do you know?" cried Frau Tischbein. She was frightfully excited and held up both her hands in anxiety.

"But he's all right, my dear — very much all right. He

has caught a thief. Think of that! And the police have presented him with a reward of a thousand marks. What do you say to that, hm? And now you must take the noon train for Berlin."

"But how do you know all that?"

"Your sister Frau Heimbold just called me up from Berlin, in the store. Emil said a few words too. And you must go right up there. As long as you have so much money, that is the thing to do."

"Yes, yes, of course," murmured Frau Tischbein distractedly. "A thousand marks? Because he caught a thief? How did he ever get that idea? He makes nothing but blunders!"

"But this one rewarded him. A thousand marks is a lot of money!"

"Oh, go on with your thousand marks!"

"Oh well, it might be worse. So you are going?"

"Naturally. I won't have a minute's peace until I've seen that boy."

"Good luck to you then, and a pleasant journey!"

"Thank you, Frau Wirth," said the hairdresser, shaking her head as she closed the door.

But when that afternoon she was seated in the train for Berlin she had another and a greater surprise. Opposite her a man was reading the paper.

Frau Tischbein's gaze flickered restlessly from one corner to the other. She counted the telegraph posts that marched past the window and would have liked to run behind the train to help push it. Time dragged so.

While she was shifting around, turning her head this way and that, she happened to glance at the paper across from her.

"Good heavens!" she cried, and snatched the paper from the man who was reading it. He thought the woman had suddenly gone mad, and was almost frightened.

"There, there!" she stammered. "That — that is my boy!" And she pointed with her finger at a photograph on the front page of the paper.

"You don't mean it?" said the man cheerfully. "You are the mother of Emil Tischbein? That's a great youngster. Hats off to you, Frau Tischbein!"

"Yes, yes," said the hairdresser. "Just keep your hat on, sir!" And then she began to read the article. Over it in giant letters was the caption:

A SMALL BOY AS DETECTIVE

HUNDREDS OF BERLIN CHILDREN CHASE A CRIMINAL

And following that came a fully detailed story of Emil's experiences from the Neustadt railway station to police headquarters in Berlin. Frau Tischbein was pale with excitement. And the paper rustled as if the wind were blowing, yet the windows were all shut tight. The man hardly could wait for her to finish the article. But it was very long — it filled almost the whole front page. And in the midst of it was Emil's picture.

Finally she laid the paper aside, looked over at the man, and said, "Such performances, the minute he's left to himself! And I warned him so carefully to look after that hundred and forty marks. How could he have been so careless? As if he didn't know that we had no money to be stolen."

"Probably he was tired out. Perhaps, even, the thief hypnotized him. That is supposed to happen," the man suggested. "But don't you think it wonderful the way the youngsters carried on the affair? That was pure genius. It was simply remarkable — simply remarkable!"

"Yes, I suppose so," answered Frau Tischbein, somewhat mollified. "He is a clever boy, my son. Always the best in his class, and always industrious. But imagine if anything had happened to him! My hair is standing on end, even though it's all over. No, I never can let him travel alone again. I'd die of worry."

"Does he look like his picture?" asked the man.

Frau Tischbein examined the picture again and said, "Yes, it's a good picture. Do you think he's nice-looking?"

"Indeed, yes!" cried the man. "Such an upstanding boy, you can expect great things from him later on."

"He should have held himself up a little straighter," fretted his mother. "His coat is full of wrinkles. He is always supposed to unbutton it before he sits down. But he never listens!"

"Well, if he has no bigger faults than that . . ." laughed the man.

"No, he hasn't any faults, really, my Emil," said his mother, as she blew her nose in an excess of emotion.

Then the man got off. She must keep his paper, and she read Emil's experiences again and again to Friedrichstrasse in Berlin. Eleven times altogether.

When they arrived in Berlin, there was Emil on the platform. In honor of his mother he had put on his best suit, and as he threw his arms around her neck he asked, "Now, what do you say to me?"

"Don't be so conceited, you monkey!"

"Well, Frau Tischbein," he said as he hooked himself onto her arm, "I certainly am tremendously glad you came."

"I see your suit hasn't been improved by your thief chasing," observed his mother, but she didn't sound very cross.

"If you want me to, I can get a new suit."

"From whom, then?"

"Oh, a clothing store wants to give me and the Professor and Gustav new suits. And then they'll announce in the paper that we detectives buy our clothes only from them. That is advertising, you understand!"

"Yes, I understand!"

"But we are probably going to refuse," Emil continued, taking big steps, "although we can each get a new football instead. You know, we think the fuss they are making over us is plain silly. The grownups can do that sort of thing, as far as we are concerned. They are funny and can't help it. But children ought to cut it out."

"Bravo!" said his mother.

"Uncle Heimbold locked up the money. A thousand marks! Isn't that great? First of all, we'll buy you an electric hair-drying machine. And then a winter coat lined with fur. And for me? I must think it over. Perhaps a new football, after all. Or maybe a camera. I'll see."

"I thought we'd better save the money and put it in the bank. Later on you can tell better what to do with it."

"No, you get the drying machine and the warm coat. What's left over we can put away, if you want to."

"We'll talk it over again," said his mother, and squeezed his arm.

"Do you know that my picture's been in all the papers? And long stories about me?"

"I read one of them in the train. At first I was worried about you. Are you sure nothing happened to you?"

"Not a thing. It was wonderful. I'll tell you all about it. But first you must meet my friends."

"Where are they, then?"

"In Schumann Street. At Aunt Martha's. She made

154

apple cake yesterday. And then we invited the whole crowd. They're up at the house now, making a racket."

Sure enough, there were great goings on at the Heimbolds'. They were all there: Gustav, the Professor, Krummbiegel, the Mittenzwey brothers, Gerold, Friedrich the First, Traugott, the little Dienstag, and all the others. There were hardly enough chairs to go around.

Pony Hütchen ran from one to the next, pouring out hot chocolate from a huge pot. And Aunt Martha's applecake was a poem. Grandmother sat on the sofa, laughing and seeming ten years younger.

When Emil came in with his mother there was a great welcome. Every boy shook hands with her. And she thanked them all for helping her Emil so much.

"And now," interrupted Emil, "the new suits and the footballs, we won't take them. We won't lend ourselves to any advertising scheme. Are we agreed?"

"Agreed," shouted Gustav, and honked his horn so that Aunt Martha's flowerpots rattled.

Then Grandmother rapped with her spoon on her gold cup, stood up, and announced, "Now, you all listen to me, you young scouts. I'm going to make a speech. But don't begin to imagine things. I am not going to praise you. The others have just about made you silly. I'm not going to do that too. I'm not going to do that too."

The boys had all become very still and did not even dare to keep on chewing.

Pony Hütchen ran from one to the other pouring chocolate.

"Chasing after a thief," went on Grandmother, "and surrounding him with a hundred children — no, that isn't a great performance. No offense meant, my friends. But there is one among you who would have liked to tiptoe after Herr Grundeis. He would have loved to spy around as the green bellboy in the hotel. But he stayed at home because he had agreed to — because he had agreed to."

Everybody looked at little Dienstag. He was blushing beet-red and was very much embarrassed.

"Quite right. I mean little Dienstag. Quite right," said Grandmother. "He sat there for two days at the telephone. He knew where his duty lay. And he did it, even though he didn't like it. That was very fine, you understand? That was very fine. You can all take an example from him. And now we'll stand up and cheer: 'Hurrah for little Dienstag!' "

The boys all jumped up. Pony Hütchen held her hands like a trumpet before her mouth. Aunt Martha and Emil's mother came in from the kitchen. And they all shouted, "Three cheers for little Dienstag!"

Then they all sat down again. And little Dienstag took a deep breath and gulped. "Thank you very much. But that's too much. You would have done it too. Any boy does what he has to. Enough! That's all."

Pony Hütchen held up the big chocolate pot and cried, "Who wants anything more to drink, you fellows? Now we'll drink to Emil!"

Eighteenth Chapter

Can Anything be Learned from It All?

L ATE IN THE AFTERNOON the boys departed. And
Emil had to promise solemnly to go to the Professor's with Pony Hütchen the very next afternoon. Then
Uncle Heimbold came in, and they had supper. After
which he gave the thousand marks to his sister-in-law,
Frau Tischbein, and advised her to put the money in
the bank.

"That was just my intention," said the hairdresser.

"No," objected Emil, "that wouldn't be any fun for
me. Mother must buy an electric drying machine and
a new coat that's lined with fur. I don't know what
you're thinking about. That money belongs to me. Can
I do what I want with it or not?"

"That you certainly cannot," declared Uncle Heimbold. "You are only a child. And the decision as to what
is to be done with the money rests with your mother."

Emil got up from the table and went over to the
window.

"Good gracious!" said Hütchen to her father. "Can't

you see that Emil was glad that he could give something to his mother? Grownups are dumb."

"Of course, she'll get the drying machine and the coat," soothed Grandmother. "But what's left over can be put in the bank, can't it, my boy?"

"Of course," agreed Emil. "Do you say so too, Mummy?"

"If you want it that way, you young millionaire."

"We'll go shopping early tomorrow," cried Emil. "Pony, you can come with us."

"Did you think, perhaps, that I'd be catching flies in the meantime?" laughed Pony. "But you must buy something for yourself, too. Of course, Aunt Tischbein must get her drying machine, but you must buy yourself a bicycle, so that you won't have to ride your cousin's bicycle to pieces."

"Emil," inquired his mother anxiously, "have you broken your cousin's bike?"

"Of course not, Mother, I only raised the handlebars a little bit higher. She always goes around bent way over like a monkey, so she'll look like a racer."

"Monkey yourself!" cried Pony. "If you change my bike again, everything's off between us, you understand?"

"If you weren't a girl, and thin as a stick besides, I'd teach you a few things, my child. Anyway, I won't bother myself about it today, but what I buy with the money or what I don't buy is none of your business." And Emil stuffed both fists in his pockets.

"Don't quarrel, don't strike, scratch each other's eyes out instead," called Grandmother soothingly, and the subject was dropped.

Later Uncle Heimbold took the dog out for an airing. That is — Heimbolds had no dog, but Pony always said that when her father went out to get his evening glass of beer.

Grandmother and the two women and Pony Hütchen and Emil sat in the living room and talked over the past few days, which had been so exciting.

"Well, perhaps the affair has it good points too," said Aunt Martha.

"Sure it has," agreed Emil. "One lesson I've learned from it: never trust anybody."

And his mother added, "I have learned that you should never let children travel alone."

"Nonsense," muttered Grandmother, "that's all wrong, all wrong."

"Nonsense! Nonsense! Nonsense!" sang Pony as she rode a chair around the room.

"You think, then, that we can't learn anything from this experience?" inquired Aunt Martha.

"Certainly," answered Grandmother.

"What, then?" they all asked in one breath.

"Never send cash, always send a money order," growled Grandmother, and chuckled like a music box.

"Hurrah!" cried Pony Hütchen, and she rode her chair into the bedroom.

ALA DELTA

Los zorros del norte

Ricardo Gómez

Ilustraciones
Ximena Maier

EDELVIVES

1

LA HISTORIA QUE TE VOY A CONTAR sucedió hace muchos, muchos años.

Tantos, que mi abuela era entonces una niña que gateaba y a mí me faltaba mucho para nacer.

Su protagonista es otra niña llamada Katrin. Pero Katrin y mi abuela no se conocieron porque vivían en países muy distantes. El país de Katrin está situado muy al norte, un lugar donde la nieve cubre los árboles durante muchos meses al año.

Está tan lejos que los patos que vienen aquí a pasar el invierno tardan semanas en llegar volando. Y tienen que descansar muchas veces antes de acabar su viaje.

Si quieres saber cómo conocí esta historia tendrás que esperar a leerla. No me la contó mi abuela, aunque ella me dio la pista.

El caso es que las historias llegan a veces de una forma sorprendente.

Te la contaré.

Y empezaré por el padre de Katrin...

2

EL PADRE DE KATRIN ERA CAZADOR. (Es decir, cazaba animales para comer su carne y curtir sus pieles.)

También era leñador.

(O sea, talaba árboles y obtenía leña para quemar en la chimenea y madera para que los carpinteros fabricasen muebles.)

Pero a Katrin no le gustaba que su padre fuese cazador ni leñador.

Prefería pensar que era barquero, porque también tenía una barca con la que cruzaba el fiordo a algunas personas que a veces pasaban por allí.

Junto con Katrin vivía su hermano pequeño, que se llamaba Hans. Y su madre.

3

LA MADRE DE KATRIN se llamaba Anna y era una madre. O sea, les criaba a ella y a su hermano pequeño, cocinaba la comida, encendía el fuego, cuidaba los animales domésticos, recogía las hortalizas del huerto, limpiaba la casa, aderezaba conservas, lavaba y cosía la ropa y procuraba que todos estuvieran felices.

(Entre otras cosas.)

Katrin no comprendía que los hombres fueran carpinteros, leñadores, cazadores o barqueros y que las madres sólo fueran madres.

Pensó que debía de haber alguna palabra para nombrar todo lo que hacían las madres.

Pero no la conocía.

Y a Katrin le gustaban mucho las palabras.

4

A KATRIN LE GUSTABAN LAS PALABRAS, pero también le gustaban otras muchas cosas. Por ejemplo, la nieve que al llegar el invierno lo cubría todo con una sábana que recordaba el azúcar.

Le gustaban los árboles, que parecían hablar, cantar o silbar cuando el viento atravesaba entre sus ramas.

Y le gustaban sobre todo los animales. Los grandes como la vaca o el caballo, que se protegían del frío en el establo. Los medianos como las ocas o las gallinas, que a veces picoteaban bajo la nieve y dormían en los gallineros. Y también los más pequeños, que vivían en el suelo o en los troncos de los árboles. Incluso los que volaban por el aire y que no parecían habitar en ningún sitio.

Por eso, a Katrin no le gustaba pensar que su padre fuera leñador ni cazador. Porque mataba animales y derribaba árboles.

Su padre tenía una escopeta.

5

LA ESCOPETA DE SU PADRE colgaba en un soporte que había encima de la chimenea.

Cuando estaba allí quieta, la escopeta no era peligrosa.

Lo malo comenzaba cuando el padre de Katrin se la echaba al hombro y salía de casa. Y lo peor llegaba cuando el padre de Katrin colocaba una bala, apuntaba y disparaba.

Entonces, sonaba un ruido terrible. Un ruido como «¡paeng!» que se extendía por el aire, cabalgaba sobre las montañas y atravesaba entre las ramas de los árboles.

Ese ruido, entonces, se convertía en un «¡páenng!».

Cuando sonaba el «¡páenng!», los árboles y los animales callaban. Porque sabían que la bala que salía de su escopeta siempre encontraba algún animal desprevenido.

Y ese animal, fuera grande o mediano, estaba perdido.

Cuando escuchaba el «¡páenng!», Katrin sentía miedo.

6

A KATRIN LE DABAN MIEDO OTRAS COSAS. Por ejemplo, las noches de invierno que eran silenciosas, porque cuando los árboles y los animales callaban era porque algo malo estaba por suceder.

(En las noches muy silenciosas podían bajar los trolls que habitan en las cumbres de las montañas.)

También le daban miedo las personas que no miraban a los ojos, porque las personas que no miran a los ojos ocultan pensamientos que no se atreven a pronunciar.

El padre de Katrin no decía muchas palabras, pero cuando hablaba o reía miraba a los ojos. Su padre sólo le daba miedo cuando se iba al bosque con la escopeta al hombro.

Y cuando regresaba con el cuerpo de algún animal, sentía además una enorme pena.

7

La pena de Katrin era como la noche. Llegaba despacio y se extendía sin hacer ruido, pero poco a poco lo llenaba todo de sombras.

La pena le comenzaba a nacer en los ojos, bajaba por su garganta, le apretaba un poco el corazón y se quedaba a dormir en su estómago.

A veces, dormía en su tripa varios días. Y durante esos días, no podía comer.

A Katrin, la pena se le pasaba despacio. No había médicos que pudieran curarla ni remedios que pudieran espantarla.

Sólo se le pasaba caminando por el bosque, escuchando cómo siseaba el viento entre los árboles o contemplando desde lejos cómo se movían los animales.

Katrin fue un día a pasear por el bosque que había cerca de su casa.

8

CERCA DE LA CASA DE KATRIN había árboles de muchas clases, pero sobre todo abetos, pinos y abedules.

(Casi todos los árboles eran enormes, pero en algunos lugares nacían retoños que algún día serían árboles grandes.)

Muchas veces, Katrin se sentaba en un claro del bosque a escucharlos.

Los árboles no hablaban, claro, pero el viento atravesaba entre sus ramas y hojas y era como si el árbol pronunciase palabras. Palabras de árbol, algunas graves y cortas como *shooo*, y otras largas y agudas como *fiumm-viuushii*.

Aunque hiciera mucho viento y hablaran a la vez, Katrin podía distinguir las voces de los abedules, de los abetos y de los pinos.

Los árboles hablaban más despacio cuando estaban cubiertos de nieve.

Ese día en que Katrin salió a pasear, todavía quedaba algo de nieve en los árboles.

9

Todavía quedaba nieve en las ramas aunque estaba a punto de llegar la primavera. En el bosque se escuchaban los sonidos del goteo de la nieve derretida: «glop, glop, glop...».

Katrin oyó un ruido distinto del «glop, glop» del agua. Se volvió hacia el lugar de donde venía ese sonido, vio pasar la cola de un animal y se dijo:

—Parece un zorro.

Buscó un lugar donde el viento no llevara su olor hasta el animal y se escondió tras un gran abeto.

Esperó pacientemente a verle de nuevo.

Pasado un rato, el animal volvió a aparecer. Tenía los pies y las orejas negras y un color gris en el resto del cuerpo. Katrin sonrió y esta vez se dijo:

—Ah... ¡es un precioso zorro plateado!

10

LOS ZORROS PLATEADOS eran raros en esas tie-
rras. Se los podía ver más al norte, en regio-
nes donde la nieve cubría la tierra todos los
meses del año.

Katrin se preguntaba:

—¿Qué hará un zorro plateado por aquí?

Y recordó una vieja leyenda. Una leyenda
que un día le contó su madre.

(Era sobre las auroras boreales, las luces
que a veces encienden el cielo y lo llenan de
colores, como si las brasas de una chimenea
gigante se hubieran esparcido por el aire.)

Según esa leyenda, un zorro plateado, hu-
yendo de los cazadores, emprendió una carre-
ra. Iba tan rápido que ascendió hasta las copas
de los árboles y las cimas de los montes. Sus
patas alzaban hacia el cielo los cristales de nieve y las Luces del Norte esparcieron por esos
cristales los colores azul, verde y rojo.

Su madre le contó esta antigua leyenda,
que ella había leído además en uno de los
libros de la casa.

11

EN LA CASA DE KATRIN HABÍA DOS LIBROS. Uno se leía sólo los domingos y era más bien extraño. A la hora de comer, su padre tomaba ese libro y leía dos o tres páginas ante toda la familia. Hasta que no acababa de leer esas páginas, no se servía la comida.

Mientras se leía ese libro tenían que estar muy callados, y Katrin no se explicaba por qué. Muchas veces no entendía lo que quería decir y le daban ganas de preguntar.

Pero su padre no dejaba que nadie preguntase. Decía que leía ese libro porque los domingos no podían ir a la iglesia.

(Su casa estaba a cuatro horas de viaje del pueblo más cercano.)

El otro libro se podía leer cualquier otro día de la semana, y a cualquier hora. Sobre todo, se lo leía su madre a ella y a su hermano.

A Katrin le gustaban las palabras que pronunciaban las personas, las que venían dentro de los libros y las casi-palabras que sonaban entre las ramas de los árboles.

Estaba recordando esto cuando, de repente, en el mismo claro del bosque vio otro animal, y se dijo:

—Ah, mira: son dos zorros.

12

DOS ZORROS CERCA DE LA CASA daban que pensar. Y, sobre todo, daban que preguntar.

«¿Qué hacen estos dos zorros por aquí? ¿Habrá otros cerca? ¿Estarán devorando algún animal muerto?»

Los animales olisquearon el aire y caminaron, uno tras otro, hacia el arroyo cercano.

Katrin salió de su escondrijo y fue hacia el lugar donde habían estado los zorros.

Le llegó un olor denso, que no era el de un animal muerto.

Buscó por los alrededores y encontró un agujero semioculto por la nieve. Pensó que los zorros debían de esconder allí su comida.

Pero del interior de aquel agujero venían algunos sonidos. Por un momento, tuvo la sensación de que se trataba de píos de pájaro.

Katrin se dijo:

—Así que tratan de devorar a los pájaros de esta nidada...

Pensó en cómo podría proteger el nido. Quizá, colocando alguna piedra, o disimulándolo con ramas...

En esto, apareció en la entrada un cachorro de zorro.

13

¡UN CACHORRITO DE ZORRO! Eso se dijo Katrin cuando vio salir de la madriguera una bola de algodón de color crema, con patas cortas y hocico rosado.

Supo que no debía tocarlo, porque las madres de muchos animales abandonan a las crías que tienen olor a humano.

Se retiró para no asustar al animal y al poco vio cómo salían del agujero otros tres zorritos. Apenas tenían los ojos abiertos.

Se dijo:

—Ah, los que han salido antes son los padres, a buscar comida para sus crías.

Katrin se retiró para que los zorritos no la siguiesen. Tras un árbol, contempló cómo los animalitos olían la entrada de la madriguera, que estaba sucia de huesos de frutos y caparazones de escarabajo.

Ahora se arrepentía de que sus pisadas hubieran quedado en el barro y en la nieve.

Katrin memorizó el lugar donde estaba la zorrera y fue corriendo hasta casa.

14

Llegó corriendo hasta su casa y su madre preguntó:

—¿Dónde estabas? Recuerda que es día de baño y me tienes que ayudar con el agua.

(Era cierto. El jueves era el día en que se bañaban. Pero ese jueves tenía muchas cosas importantes que hacer.)

—Un momento, mamá. Tengo que hacer una cosa muy importante.

Katrin fue a la cocina y tomó un pedazo de pan reseco que mojó en leche. Después, buscó un par de peras muy maduras y un puñado de fresas. Lo puso todo en un cuenco y salió corriendo de casa. Tranquilizó a su madre:

—Ahora vuelvo y me ocupo del agua.

Katrin volcó el contenido del cuenco en los alrededores de la zorrera. No era mucho, pero pensó que al día siguiente se las apañaría para llevar algo más de comida.

Volvió a casa corriendo. Tenía que ayudar a su madre a preparar el baño.

15

Preparar el baño resultaba entretenido. Además, era un placer sentir el agua caliente en la piel.

Su madre había puesto a la lumbre el primer caldero. Katrin ayudaba llevando cubos de agua. Cuando el agua hervía, se echaba en el enorme balde de zinc que hacía de bañera.

Anna comenzó con el niño. Mezcló el agua caliente y la fría para buscar la temperatura adecuada y metió dentro al pequeño Hans, a quien frotó con un jabón que olía a campo.

Cuando hubo un par de calderos calientes, le tocó el turno a Katrin, que se desnudó y se dejó restregar por su madre.

Katrin se habría quedado toda la mañana en el baño, pero el agua se enfriaba y le llegaba el turno a la madre.

Anna se desvistió y se metió en el balde. Su hija le restregó la espalda y la ayudó a aclararse el jabón del cuerpo.

A Katrin le gustaba ver a su madre desnuda. Pensó que algún día sería como ella.

Su padre nunca se bañaba los jueves. Solía hacerlo los viernes por la noche, cuando Katrin y Hans estaban dormidos.

16

Hans y Katrin estaban todavía dormidos cuando a la mañana siguiente se oyeron ruidos fuera de la casa.

Era su padre, que gritaba a la puerta del gallinero, mientras se oía el alboroto de las ocas y de las gallinas.

Katrin se asomó afuera y encontró a su padre de muy mal humor:

—¡Seguro que es un zorro! Se ha llevado una de las gallinas.

En el suelo, Katrin pudo ver algunas plumas, junto con unas gotas de sangre. Y unas huellas que se perdían hacia el bosque.

Su padre aseguraba:

—Estas pisadas son de zorro. No cabe duda.

Katrin miró preocupada el destrozo e imaginó que lo que iba a suceder no sería nada, nada bueno.

Anna también estaba abatida al pensar que los animales de la granja estaban en peligro.

Sólo Hans parecía no darse cuenta de lo que ocurría, pues jugaba divertido, recogiendo plumas del suelo.

Mientras desayunaba, Katrin sintió a la vez miedo y pena, cuando vio que su padre tomaba la escopeta de encima de la chimenea.

Y se sintió además muy culpable.

17

Se sintió muy culpable al pensar que los zorros habían seguido sus huellas hasta la casa y que eso les llevó hasta el gallinero.

Katrin pasó la mañana practicando la lectura con su madre y ayudando a dar de comer a los animales. También peló patatas y, cuando estuvieron cocidas, se encargó de rellenarlas de verduras.

Pero sobre todo pensaba en su padre. Y en los dos zorros que cuidaban a los zorritos.

Ella era la responsable del desastre que iba a suceder.

En un momento, llegó un ruido conocido y que venía rodando por las montañas: «¡páenng!».

Y al rato otro: «¡páenng!».

Katrin imaginó a los dos zorros muertos. Eso significaba que su camada no sobreviviría.

¡Y ella tenía la culpa de todo!

Cuando ya era casi la hora de comer, su padre apareció.

18

EL PADRE DE KATRIN APARECIÓ con rostro preo-
cupado. Dejó la escopeta sobre la chimenea
y se sentó a la mesa.

Katrin pensó que su padre no había que-
rido entrar con los cuerpos de los zorros y
salió para ver si los había dejado fuera.

No vio nada.

Y sitió una enorme alegría, como si le
desanudaran el estómago, cuando le oyó:

—¡Malditos zorros! Se me han escapado.
Tendré que salir mañana a por ellos.

(Era la primera vez que un disparo de su
padre no acababa con un animal. No era
raro que estuviese de tan mal humor.)

Por la tarde, Katrin ayudó a su padre a co-
ser la malla del gallinero. Tenía la esperanza
de convencerle de no salir tras los zorros:

—Habrán huido al oír los disparos. Ya
verás como no vuelven por aquí.

—Volverán, hija. Un zorro siempre vuelve
al lugar donde ha encontrado comida.

19

Volvieron a la noche siguiente.

Aunque no lograron entrar en el gallinero, rompieron una tabla de la despensa y alcanzaron el estante donde estaban las manzanas. Muchas estaban mordisqueadas.

El padre de Katrin volvió a descolgar la escopeta y, esta vez, metió más de dos balas en sus bolsillos. La niña le vio marcharse, lleno de furia, en busca de los zorros.

¡Esta vez sí que estaban perdidos!

Mientras la pena le bajaba por la garganta, le ataba el corazón y se quedaba en su estómago, Katrin no hacía más que pensar en los zorritos.

Se oyó un «¡páenng!».

Luego otro «¡páenng!».

Y un tercero.

Su padre regresó dos horas más tarde. Estaba pálido. No quiso hablar del asunto, pero ni a la entrada ni fuera de la casa había rastro de los cuerpos de los zorros.

¿Sería posible...?

Por la tarde, Katrin dijo que se iba a pasear.

20

Y PASEÓ ENTRE LOS ABEDULES, los abetos y los pinos, con el corazón encogido y un nudo en la tripa.

Llegó a la madriguera y vio que había sido abandonada. No encontró rastro de los zorritos, ni de mamá zorra ni de papá zorro.

Sin embargo, Katrin dejó en aquel lugar un montoncito de judías verdes, castañas secas y manzanas mordisqueadas.

Volvió dando un rodeo, procurando pisar las piedras para que los zorros no siguieran sus huellas y no se acercaran a la casa.

Antes de caer la noche, su padre había revisado el gallinero, arreglado la puerta de la despensa y atrancado el granero.

Katrin le vio contento y no supo por qué.

Pero después de cenar se enteró. Su padre vació cerca del sendero un saco de patatas y zanahorias viejas.

Luego, tomó la escopeta, se abrigó para pasar la noche fuera de casa y buscó un lugar escondido donde vigilar la senda.

¡Estaba dispuesto a tenderles una trampa!

Katrin no entendía que su padre fuera tan cruel con esos pobres animales. Total, por unas manzanas y una pobre gallina…

Apenas pudo dormir.

21

PASÓ CASI TODA LA NOCHE SIN DORMIR tratando de enviar un mensaje a los zorros. Un consejo a distancia.

El mensaje decía: «¡No vengáis, no vengáis, no vengáis, no vengáis...!».

A Katrin le hubiera gustado poder hablar con los árboles para que éstos transmitieran el aviso: «No vengáis, no vengáis...».

Y, como si los árboles la hubieran escuchado, los zorros no aparecieron.

Por lo menos, cuando amaneció no se había oído ningún disparo.

Katrin nunca había visto a su padre de tan mal humor. Cuando ella preguntó por los zorros él no le miró a la cara al responder:

—¡No han aparecido! ¡Los muy zorros...!

Las patatas y las zanahorias viejas habían quedado a la puerta de la casa. Katrin las recogió y las volvió a meter en el saco.

Esa mañana, su padre no salió de caza.

Durante unas horas, paseó de acá para allá, mirando el bosque y rumiando su venganza.

Y por la tarde, de la rabia que sentía, tomó el hacha y cortó un pino. Un pino que no necesitaba, porque en la leñera había madera suficiente.

Una vez más, a Katrin no le gustó que su padre fuera cazador.

Y tampoco leñador.

22

Los leñadores no ven los árboles igual que los ven otras personas, pensaba Katrin. Lo había comprobado en ocasiones.

A veces, su padre y otros leñadores miraban un árbol y decían:

—Éste será bueno para hacer una mesa.

O:

—Éste es el mejor para fabricar una barca.

En lugar de decir «Qué copa tan alta tiene», o «Cómo suena el viento en sus hojas», o «Hay que ver cuántos pájaros duermen en él».

Ni siquiera pedían perdón al árbol por talar su tronco. Se liaban, «¡zas, zas!», y lo cortaban.

Peor todavía era cazar animales.

Los animales estaban tan tranquilos y, de pronto, «¡bang!». No tendrían ni tiempo de oír el ruido.

Katrin pensó que, de mayor, ella nunca se casaría con un leñador ni con un cazador.

Si acaso, con un barquero...

Esa tarde, alguien apareció por allí. Llevaba una escopeta al hombro y preguntó al padre:

—¿Es suya la barca del embarcadero?

Se lo preguntó sin mirarle a la cara.

A Katrin, ese hombre no le gustó.

23

ESE HOMBRE NO LE GUSTÓ porque no miraba a la cara, pero también por su escopeta de dos cañones y por la conversación que mantuvo con su padre:

—Ayer oí muchos disparos.

—Sí.

—Habrá buena caza por aquí.

—Sí. Pero además hay un zorro... Puede que incluso dos o más.

—¿Zorros? Podemos organizar una batida. Entre dos cazadores...

Cuando su padre le invitó a dormir en casa, la niña supo que a su madre tampoco le gustaba ese forastero.

De madrugada, su padre y el forastero agarraron las escopetas, se llenaron el zurrón de balas y cartuchos y salieron a cazar.

Katrin, que casi no había dormido y que tenía un retortijón en la tripa, se asomó por la puerta de su habitación para ver salir a los dos hombres.

Anna se levantó poco más tarde. Se sorprendió al ver a su hija levantada:

—Pero, hija, ¿qué haces? Vas a agarrar un resfriado. Ven, que te preparo el desayuno.

—No tengo hambre.

24

CUANDO KATRIN NO TENÍA HAMBRE no servía de nada insistir. Su madre lo sabía, y sospechaba que su hija estaba apenada por algo. Le preguntó por qué.

La niña le contó el encuentro con los zorros y con los zorritos en la madriguera.

—Si no están sus padres, esos animales morirán... ¡Y no quiero que papá los mate!

Incluso Anna sintió un picotazo en el estómago cuando escuchó a su hija. Y se le quitaron las ganas de desayunar.

Katrin salió a pasear.

Mientras paseaba comenzó a pedir a los zorros, como si pudieran escucharla y como si pudieran entenderla:

—Por favor, escondeos. Escondeos bien.

(Aunque Katrin, claro, sabía que los zorros estaban muy lejos para poder oírla, y que aunque anduvieran cerca no entenderían sus palabras).

Y luego dijo a un árbol, como si pudiera oírla y pudiera comprenderla:

—Por favor, árbol, si puedes esconderlos, escóndelos. Lleva el mensaje a otros árboles.

(Pero el árbol, claro, no respondió. Sólo podía agitar sus hojas al viento y dejar que cayera la nieve que se fundía en sus ramas: «glop, glop, glop...».)

En esto, se oyó un «¡pouuum!».

25

La niña sospechó que ese «¡POUUUM!» era el ruido de la escopeta del forastero, que llegaba hasta allí trepando como un ruido gordo y feo por la ladera de la montaña.

Pero no tuvo tiempo de pensar en mucho más porque al poco oyó un «¡páenng!».

Katrin comenzó a correr en dirección a los disparos. Corrió, tropezó y se cayó una vez en un nevero, mojándose parte del cuerpo.

Se dirigió a un árbol cercano y suplicó:

—Por favor, abeto, si puedes ayudarles, ayuda a los zorros. Y avisa a otros árboles...

De nuevo sonó un «¡po-pouum!» de la escopeta de doble cañón del forastero.

Y a continuación otro «¡páenng!».

A pesar de esos sucios ruidos, que ocultaban los sonidos del viento en el bosque, Katrin sintió cierta alegría. Eso significaba que los dos zorros no eran fáciles de cazar.

Entonces, sucedió algo curioso.

Katrin observó el cielo...

26

KATRIN MIRÓ AL CIELO y vio varias bandadas de pájaros. Pensó que, asustadas, las aves huían de las ramas de los árboles de la zona.

(Porque en ese bosque nunca se habían oído tantos disparos a la vez.)

Las escopetas seguían disparando y los pájaros volaban de un lado a otro, sin saber bien en qué rama posarse.

Katrin nunca había visto tantos pájaros juntos. Unos, pequeños y plateados, volaban sobre las copas de los árboles. Otros, negros y gordos, planeaban cerca de las cumbres.

Como si los pájaros agitaran el aire, el viento empezó a soplar. Era un viento helado, que silbaba agudo entre las ramas de los abedules, los abetos y los pinos.

Por fin, el cielo se oscureció y comenzó a llover. Primero, un agua fina y fría, que claveteaba el rostro. Después, un agua gorda y cálida, que empapaba la ropa.

A partir de ese momento, sólo se oyó un «¡puuuum!».

Luego, vino el silencio, tras el cual Katrin tuvo un mal presagio.

Aterida bajo las ramas de un pino, deseó escuchar otro disparo. Pero sólo llegó un silencio largo y pesado, roto por el susurro del viento en los árboles («sshuiiu») y por el tableteo de las gotas en las hojas y en el suelo («clap, tataclap, taclap...»).

Pasado el tiempo, Katrin echó a correr en dirección a casa.

27

Cuando llegó a casa, la madre esperaba a la puerta. Al ver llegar a su hija empapada, salió hacia ella:

—Pero ¿dónde te has metido? Estaba tan preocupada... Ven. Te vas a resfriar.

Katrin dejó que su madre le quitase la ropa adherida a su piel. Y se dejó secar y frotar con la manta que le echó por encima.

Su hermano Hans, sentado en el suelo, miraba la escena con ojos divertidos.

Aunque no tenía hambre, Katrin aceptó tomar una taza de caldo, que le calentó por dentro pero que no le quitó la tiritona.

A la hora del almuerzo no quiso comer. No pensaba más que en los pobres zorritos. Y en que su padre no le había mirado a la cara.

Su madre sacó el colchón de su cama, lo tendió en la sala y encendió la chimenea.

Los tres pasaron allí la tarde. Katrin y Hans se tumbaron en el colchón y se taparon con la manta, mientras su madre les leía el libro de todos los días.

En el tejado repiqueteaba la lluvia. A través de las paredes se escuchaba el silbido del viento entre los árboles.

De vez en cuando, Anna se asomaba a la ventana. Katrin sabía que estaba esperando a su padre. No había vuelto y casi era de noche.

28

CASI ERA DE NOCHE Y SU PADRE aún no había regresado. Katrin notó que su madre estaba intranquila.

Aunque la lluvia por fin había amainado, ya no escucharon ningún otro disparo en el bosque.

Sólo cenó el pequeño Hans, porque Anna y Katrin tenían un nudo en el estómago.

Cuando pasaron las horas y la noche envolvió la casa, Anna colocó un candil en la ventana. Hans se había dormido y Katrin y su madre se miraron sin saber qué decir.

(Su padre nunca había vuelto tan tarde a casa sin avisar.)

Cerca de las doce, Anna se puso un abrigo y salió a los alrededores de la casa. Gritó:

—¡Halmar! ¡Halmaaaar!

Nadie respondió a su llamada.

Los ojos de Anna y de su hija trataban de disimular la angustia, pero no lo conseguían.

Al calor de la chimenea y alumbradas por un par de candiles, las dos tomaron un libro.

Anna, el de los domingos. Katrin, el otro. Pero ninguna estaba pendiente de lo que leía.

Las dos se sobresaltaron al oír algo parecido a un llanto a la entrada de la casa.

29

Parecía un llanto, como de niño, pero al abrir la puerta encontraron unos ojos de color escarlata. Era la zorra, que emitía un gruñido parecido a un:

—Iññ, iññ.

El animal movía su larga cola plateada. Katrin gritó a su madre:

—¡Es la zorra! La que vi en el bosque...

—¿Y qué hace aquí?

El animal gruñía, agitando su cola y girándose hacia el camino. Miraba a las dos mujeres y señalaba el sendero.

Katrin comprendió:

—¡Quiere que la sigamos!

—¿Para qué?

—No lo sé, pero parece que quiere decir algo.

Las mujeres se miraron sin comprender. ¿Ese animal pedía ayuda para sus crías? ¿Y dónde estaba el zorro? ¿Y su padre?

Katrin dijo a su madre:

—Me está pidiendo ayuda. Voy a seguirla.

—¡Ni hablar! No saldrás esta noche... y menos sin estar tu padre aquí.

—Pero a lo mejor sabe dónde está papá...

—Iré yo. Tú cuida de Hans.

—No, yo quiero ir... A mí me conoce.

La zorra seguía gruñendo y señalando el camino, cada vez más nerviosa.

Al fin, Anna despertó a Hans...

30

La madre despertó a Hans y le dijo:

—Hans. Te vas a quedar solo un rato. No tengas miedo porque Katrin y yo volveremos pronto. ¿De acuerdo?

El niño miró a su madre y a su hermana con ojos somnolientos. Katrin se alegró al pensar que su hermano era un chico muy valiente.

Prepararon un candil, se pusieron los abrigos y salieron fuera. Al ver la luz, el animal se asustó y comenzó a recular, pero Katrin le tranquilizó acariciando su lomo:

—No temas. Te acompañaremos.

La zorra tomó el sendero y Anna y Katrin la siguieron. El candil proyectaba ante ellas una esfera de luz, pero no podían evitar que sus pies chapotearan entre los charcos.

El animal caminaba pendiente de las mujeres. Avanzaba, echaba la vista atrás, se detenía y gruñía suavemente para guiarlas por el sonido:

—Iññ, iññ, iññ...

Se internaron en el bosque. Los árboles rezumaban agua. Al goteo de las ramas se unían los susurros de los regatos en el suelo.

Subieron por una cuesta y volvieron a bajar. Katrin suponía que iban hacia el arroyo.

El rumor del agua era cada vez más intenso. La zorra se detuvo y comenzó a husmear. Lanzó varios gruñidos y al poco se oyó un ladrido suave:

—Ggau, ggau...

Anna acercó la luz. En el hueco de un viejo tronco, el zorro protegía a su camada, que rebullía al fondo. La zorra se acercó y lamió al macho en el lomo y cerca del cuello. Katrin vio manchas de sangre.

—¡Mira! Está herido... Hay que curarle.

Pero el zorro se alzó sobre sus patas. Lamió la boca de la hembra y ésta se recostó junto a los cachorros, dejándoles que se prendieran de sus pezones.

El macho salió del hueco y comenzó a caminar, cojeando y gruñendo. Al igual que antes había hecho la hembra, agitaba la cola y esperaba que las mujeres lo siguiesen. Katrin convenció a su madre:

—Vamos a seguirle.

Agarraron de nuevo el candil y siguieron al animal, que tomó un camino escarpado, hacia el fondo del arroyo. Katrin y su madre resbalaban sobre el barro y los arbustos.

Esperanzada al pensar que el animal les dirigía hacia su marido, la madre gritó:

—¡Halmar! ¡Halmaaaar!

Al borde del agua, el ruido era tan intenso que apenas podían oír nada. Pero la mujer siguió gritando:

—¡Halmaaar! ¡Halmaaaaaaaar!

El zorro iba muy despacio. Su ladrido se había convertido en un gruñido suave:

—Ggn, ggnn.

Al final, el animal se sentó en el suelo. Katrin lo acarició y su mano se tiñó de sangre. El zorro se incorporó de nuevo, para volver a caer a los pocos pasos.

Katrin se quedó con él.

La madre continuó gritando mientras seguía con el candil el curso del arroyo:

—¡Halmaaar!

De pronto, oyó una débil voz:

—Anna, Anna... Aquí...

Halmar estaba tendido junto al agua, con una pierna encajada entre dos piedras. Sus ropas y su rostro estaban cubiertos de barro.

—Halmar... ¿estás bien?

—Creo que sí... Pero necesito ayuda...

—Sí, cariño, ya estamos aquí. Te ayudaré a sacar el pie.

—No, no puedes. La roca es muy pesada. Debes buscar la escopeta. Estará por ahí...

Anna la buscó por los alrededores. Tardó en encontrarla pero al final vino con ella. Hizo lo que Halmar le indicaba, utilizándola como palanca para apartar la roca. Al final, tras muchos esfuerzos, la movió lo bastante para que el hombre liberara su pie.

Halmar y su mujer se abrazaron. Él preguntó:

—¿Cómo me habéis encontrado?

—Ya te lo contaré. Katrin está por ahí arriba. ¿Y el hombre que iba contigo?

—Me abandonó. Cuando llegó la riada y me caí, me dejó aquí. No quería más que la piel de esos animales. Cuando vio que no podía cazarlos se puso como loco y me robó el zurrón. El que tú me regalaste.

—Ya te decía que ese hombre no me gustaba. Vamos...

Utilizando el arma como muleta, con la culata encajada en la axila y el cañón apoyado en el suelo, Halmar logró llegar donde estaba Katrin. Ésta se abrazó a su padre:

—¡Papá, papá! ¿Estás bien...?

—Sí, hija. ¡Qué alegría veros! Este tiempo he pensado mucho en vosotras y en Hans. Os quiero mucho a los tres.

De repente, Halmar vio que un zorro alzaba la cabeza a pocos pasos y preguntó sobresaltado:

—¿Y ese animal? ¿Qué está haciendo aquí? ¿Dónde están mis balas?

La niña le dio unas palmadas en el brazo y le tranquilizó:

—Ya te contaré, papá.

Katrin se agachó hasta donde estaba el animal, que ahora parecía dormir.

(El padre comenzó a sospechar que ese era el zorro que había intentado cazar y comenzó a sentirse bastante avergonzado.)

Iniciaron un penoso camino de ascenso. Anna sostenía a su marido mientras éste se apoyaba en la escopeta, que hundía su cañón en el fango. Katrin llevaba encima al zorro, sintiendo que poco a poco el calor del animal se escapaba de su cuerpo.

Llegaron a donde estaban la hembra y los zorritos. Esta vez fue la niña quien invitó a la hembra:

—¡Ven! ¡Ven con nosotros!

Al ver que la zorra no se movía, Katrin se agachó y le mostró la cabeza del macho. Ella gimió con lo que parecían unos hipos, «iñ-iñ-iñ», mientras lamía la boca de su compañero. Al final se alzó y siguió a la niña, después de poner en pie con el hocico a sus crías.

Los zorritos iniciaron lo que para ellos fue un larguísimo camino, azuzados por su madre, que los hocicaba para ayudarles. A mitad del viaje parecían bolitas de barro arrastrándose por el fango.

Katrin apretaba el cuerpo del zorro contra el suyo tratando de darle calor, mientras le susurraba al oído una y otra vez:

—Gracias por salvar a mi papá. Ya verás como te pones bien. Gracias por salvarle...

Los árboles siguieron soltando su «glop-glop» mientras algunos pájaros nocturnos se asustaron al ver esa extraña procesión.

Al fin, llegaron a casa...

31

EN LA CASA, las brasas de la chimenea pintaban las paredes y los escasos muebles con un color rojizo. Chorreando agua y fango, Halmar, Anna y Katrin entraron y se acercaron al fuego. La niña cargaba el cuerpo del zorro y lo dejó con cuidado sobre la alfombra de piel.

A la puerta, la zorra no hacía más que gemir, sin atreverse a entrar. Tras ella, los cuatro cachorros estaban agotados y helados.

—Lo primero es cambiarse de ropa...

Eso dijo la madre de Katrin. Pero la niña intentaba convencer a la zorra de que pasase. Le señalaba el cuerpo del macho y le decía:

—Pasa, pasa. Aquí podrás cuidarlo...

La hembra, pasito a pasito, entró en la sala y, cuando vio al zorro, comenzó a lamerle la cara y a gemir.

Mientras Anna iba a por mantas y toallas y trataba de desnudar a su marido, Katrin fue a por los cachorros y, uno a uno, los puso junto a sus padres.

Hans se despertó en ese momento...

32

HANS SE DESPERTÓ y vio a su padre desnudo, a varios animales tendidos en la alfombra y a su madre y a su hermana cubiertos de barro. Lo miró todo con ojos asombrados.

Anna se limpió la cara y trató de convencer al niño:

—Anda, hijo, vete a la cama. Esto es como un sueño. Mañana te lo explicaremos.

Pero Hans no estaba dispuesto a perderse esa escena. Buscó un lugar tibio delante de la chimenea y disfrutó despierto de lo que, efectivamente, parecía un sueño.

(A Hans no le gustaban las palabras tanto como a su hermana Katrin, pero disfrutaba siempre que había un espectáculo inusual.)

Al día siguiente...

33

Al día siguiente, Katrin comprobó que la lluvia cálida de la víspera había derretido toda la nieve que quedaba en los árboles.

Era como si por fin hubiera llegado la primavera. Pronto, todo se llenaría de flores y de frutos y los árboles podrían hablar más claro, sin el peso de la nieve en sus ramas.

Salió fuera de la casa y dijo:

—Gracias, árboles, gracias por ayudarnos.

Anna había partido muy temprano al pueblo vecino para traer al médico.

(Regresaron por la tarde, pues el pueblo vecino estaba bastante alejado.)

El doctor entablilló el pie de Halmar y le aconsejó que estuviera dos semanas en reposo. Dijo que no parecía tener fractura, pero que nunca se sabía...

Luego, recomendó que los tres se prepararan un buen jarabe con azúcar y zumo de grosellas y que hicieran infusiones con hojas de abedul, para prevenir el resfriado.

A Hans, que no quería ser menos que los demás, también le recetó unos zumos de fresa, la fruta que más le gustaba.

Accedió a continuación a ocuparse del zorro, a quien extrajo con unas pinzas dos perdigones del cuello y del lomo. Le desinfectó la herida y cosió con cuidado su piel.

Y por último, el doctor se invitó a cenar con la familia, para que le contaran esa extraordinaria historia de los dos zorros que habían salvado la vida de un vecino.

El niño jugueteó con los cachorros todo el día. Los lavó con mimo, acarició su piel y disfrutó viendo cómo mamaban de su madre. La zorra le dejó sobar a las crías, quizá convencida de que, en el fondo, esos humanos no eran tan peligrosos.

Al médico, lo que vio y lo que le contaron le pareció increíble.

34

LE PARECIÓ INCREÍBLE NO SÓLO AL MÉDICO, sino también a los vecinos del pueblo, que no acababan de creer que unos zorros hubieran salvado la vida de una persona.

Así que se preguntaban unos a otros queriendo saber si la historia era cierta, y visitaban al médico, que les contaba además:

—Si vais a casa de Halmar veréis que encima de la chimenea tiene una escopeta roñosa y con el cañón torcido. No la ha vuelto a utilizar y si habláis con él os asegurará que no volverá a cazar ningún animal.

—Los zorros desaparecieron un día sin dejar rastro. Los seis. La misma noche que se fueron, sobre las montañas que siempre están cubiertas de nieve, las Luces del Norte esparcieron sus colores rojo, verde y azul.

—Parece que la niña es algo especial. Dice que habla con los árboles y yo ni me lo creo ni me lo dejo de creer. Pero el caso es que una vez...

Y estas historias y otras que vienen de un país situado muy al norte, donde la nieve cubre los bosques muchos meses al año, se contaron una y otra vez.

35

Se contaron una y otra vez.

Un paciente del médico se la contó a un vecino del pueblo de al lado. Éste se la contó a un pescador, que se la pasó a un vendedor de perfumes, que contó la historia a una mujer que tenía una verruga en la nariz, que se la contó a un actor de teatro que estaba enamorado de ella, que se la contó a un carretero que vendía quesos, que se la contó a un fabricante de bicicletas, que se la contó un día de excursión a un montañero, que se la contó a una enfermera que le cuidó en una caída, que se la contó a un faquir que actuaba en un café de París, (...), que se la contó a una taquillera, que se la contó a su marido, que se la contó a un telegrafista, que se la contó a un fotógrafo, que se la contó a una chica que posaba para él, que se la contó a su tía periodista, que se la contó a un saltimbanqui, que se la contó a un cuidador de palomas mensajeras que fue novio de mi abuela...

Y un día me dijo mi abuela:

—Pues un antiguo novio, un día se enteró de una historia increíble.

Fui a verle. Le pregunté. Me la contó.

Y ahora yo te la cuento a ti.

(Palabra más, palabrita menos.)